the
Drake
equation

the Drake equation

by Bart King

DISN**E**Y • HYPERION

Los Angeles   New York

All rights reserved. Published by Disney • Hyperion, an imprint of Disney Book Group. No part of this book may be reproduced or transmitted in any form or by any means, electronic or mechanical, including photocopying, recording, or by any information storage and retrieval system, without written permission from the publisher. For information address Disney • Hyperion, 125 West End Avenue, New York, New York 10023.

Printed in the United States of America
First Edition, May 2016
1 3 5 7 9 10 8 6 4 2
FAC-020093-16046

Library of Congress Cataloging-in-Publication Data
King, Bart
    The Drake Equation / by Bart King.—First edition.
        pages cm
    Summary: "Noah Grow is a birdwatcher who is on a quest to find a wood duck, but instead finds a strange, bedazzled disc. Noah and his best friends, Jason and Jenny, soon discover that the mysterious disc gives Noah peculiar powers. As things go from odd to outrageous, Noah is swept up in a storm of intergalactic intrigue and middle school mayhem."—Provided by publisher.
    ISBN 978-1-4847-2552-8 (hardcover)
    [1. Bird watching—Fiction. 2. Schools—Fiction. 3. Science fiction.] I. Title.
    PZ7.1.K585Dr 2016
    [E]—dc23   2015019783

Visit www.DisneyBooks.com

To Peter

the Drake equation

1

IMAGINE IT'S THE MIDDLE OF THE NIGHT.

And you're *way* out in the wilderness. I mean, it's so dark, you can't even see your hand in front of your face. (Or your foot, if you're really flexible.)

Above you is a deep black sky, with a sweep of glittering stars. And for some weird reason, there are rows and rows of dominoes around you.

Look, just play along, okay?

Some of the rows are short, while others lead far off into the distance. Step one way, and you'll knock over one domino. Step a different way, and you'll knock over another domino. Then *that* domino will hit another one, and so on and so on and so on. . . .

Life is sort of like this. It's hard to see where we're going when we're always in the dark.

Take me, for example. This week, I started an avalanche of dominoes. People went to the hospital. My school was nearly destroyed. I had a strange adventure with peanut butter. And *most* amazingly—

Well, I'll get to that. But guess what earth-shattering act of mine caused all these disasters?

I got off at the wrong bus stop.

As usual, I was riding the school bus home. As usual, I was sitting next to Ronnie Ramirez.

And as usual, Ronnie was wearing dress pants.

RONNIE RAMIREZ *(Balbuttio stuteris)*

APPEARANCE: Dark-haired. Slightly chunky. Eyes bulge a bit from head.

VOICE: Frequently repeats consonants and vowels.

RANGE/SOCIAL BEHAVIOR: Girls call Ronnie "adorable," which gives him access to a wider range of cliques than would normally be the case.

STATUS: Despite no defensive abilities, not endangered.

PLUMAGE: Dress pants.

Why does Ronnie wear dress pants? I don't know. Like the dominoes, it's just one of life's great mysteries.

It was a hot afternoon. As the bus climbed Pleasant Ridge Road, the heat lulled me into a daydream. So my head was just sort of bouncing against the window when there was a raucous crow of laughter from behind me.

Someone was getting teased, but I didn't turn around to look. Instead, I glanced over at Ronnie—calm, defenseless Ronnie, who was currently picking his nose.

How does he do it? I wondered.

Ronnie saw me looking at him, so he quickly removed his finger from his nose and tried to look innocent.

"How do you do it?" I asked him.

"D-do this?" Ronnie asked, holding up his finger.

"I know how to pick my nose, Ronnie," I said impatiently. "I'm wondering why you never get picked *on*."

Ronnie looked genuinely surprised. "But why would someone p-pick on me?"

"You're pretty small," I answered. "And you're almost as bad at sports as I am."

Monique Wilson leaned forward from the seat behind us. She always sits there. Monique's claim to fame was inhaling a piece of banana at lunch last year and then turning a weird color.

"Plus, Ronnie, you stutter," she pointed out helpfully. "Noah's right. You really *should* get picked on more."

Ronnie pursed his lips thoughtfully. "Well, m-maybe there

is *one* reason it doesn't happen," he said. "I try to never, ever argue with p-people."

"What? How would *that* matter?" Monique demanded.

"You're r-right," Ronnie said agreeably. "That can't be it."

Monique and I rolled our eyes at each other, and the bus wheezed to a stop. Our school is K–8. That means seventh graders like us ride home with younger life-forms—like the third graders who were standing to get off.

And as the bus door swung open, I heard a high-pitched sound that changed my life forever:

Hoo-wett! Hoo-wett!

It may sound bizarre, but I was pretty sure that call was made by a duck. Yeah, I know it wasn't a quack, but lots of duck species *don't* quack. Instead, they whistle, burp, chirp, squeak, purr, grunt, bray, honk, groan, and growl. And male ducks, called drakes, often make a completely different sound from the females. Like, if you ever hear a duck make a classic "quack" sound, it's probably a female. (Drakes aren't big quackers.)

Anyway, after the *Hoo-wett! Hoo-wett!* call, there was a thin, high whistle, like someone had just stepped on a squeaky toy. I was also pretty sure only *one* duck makes that sound—the male wood duck! I hadn't ever seen one, so my American Birding Association checklist looked like this:

☐ Wood duck *(Aix sponsa)*

See how the box isn't checked off? That kind of thing's really annoying.

So yeah, I'm a bird-watcher.[1] And I know what you're thinking: you think I'm some kid in a floppy hat, peering up into trees through my binoculars.

If so, good job—that's *exactly* what I do!

Anyway—there I was on the hot school bus. And after hearing what might've been a wood duck, I made a quick decision. Grabbing my backpack, I stood up.

"W-where are you going, Noah?" Ronnie asked.

"Just checking something out," I said. "See ya tomorrow."

Now, remember what I said about being surrounded by invisible dominoes? As I walked to the front of the bus, I knocked one of them over. I just didn't know it yet.

Mr. Berry, the bus driver, glanced at me. "Takin' a field trip?"

"Just today," I said. "I can walk home from here."

---

1. FIELD NOTES: About Me (Yay, Me)

My family moved to Santa Rosa three years ago. It's a city in northern California that's twenty miles from the ocean. Before that I lived my whole life in Albuquerque, New Mexico—up in the mountains, and nowhere near the sea.

The first thing I did after we moved was unpack my binoculars so I could start identifying new bird species. I doubted any local kids would be birders, but theorized that my scientific outlook might impress the neighborhood adults.

This theory was tested when I was sitting in our front yard, scanning the trees. Next door, I heard our neighbors, Mr. and Mrs. Shuey, come out on their porch.

"Look," Mrs. Shuey whispered loudly. "There's that new boy with the binoculars again. Do you think he's . . . ?" Her voice trailed off, so I swung my binocular view over to their porch. That gave me a nice close-up of Mrs. Shuey tapping her head, like "cuckoo."

Conclusion: The neighborhood adults were not impressed.

I looked out the bus door. From high up on Pleasant Ridge, I could see my whole neighborhood. The thing is, I don't actually live very far from Robert F. Moral School. I could ride my bike there, or even walk. But I take the school bus for my own safety. (You'll see what I mean by that in a second.)

Stepping down off the bus, I kept my eyes on the trees, hoping to catch a lucky glimpse of my bird. (Unlike most duck species, wood ducks like to perch in trees.) And so I *didn't* see the deep pothole in front of me—until I stepped right into it.

Rolling my ankle (*"Ouch!"*), I stumbled and started to fall. But by waving my arms around like a lunatic (*"Whoooa! Whoooa!"*), I lurched wildly around and somehow kept my balance.

Finally I stopped staggering and got my footing back.

"Whew!" I said to myself in relief. "Close call."

I glanced up at the bus to see a bunch of the first graders in the front seats squealing with laughter and pointing at me. One was waving his arms around, making funny faces, and going, *"Whoooa! Whoooa!"*

Know what's bad for your self-esteem? Having little kids make fun of you.

Hoo-wett! Hoo-wett!

The wood duck! I instantly forgot about the first graders, spun around, and grabbed my binoculars out of my backpack. (Yes, I carry binoculars with me.) I barely noticed as Mr. Berry closed the bus doors behind me.

Oh, hang on. I forgot to finish explaining what the big deal is with the wood ducks. See, I'd actually been thinking about those ducks a lot. Here, maybe this shortened version of my sixth-grade science fair project will help explain:

The Drake Equation:

An Ongoing Experiment

by Noah Grow

OVERVIEW: Santa Rosa's wetlands were once home to a healthy wood duck population. Over the last twenty years, their numbers have sunk about 4 percent annually. Today, only a few wood ducks are left in Santa Rosa, and experts—okay, I— believe this is due to three factors:

☐ Cutting down trees (wood ducks perch and nest in trees)

☐ Draining wetlands for construction (wood ducks like wet, forested areas)

☐ Illegally hunting male wood ducks, "drakes" (wood ducks have pretty cool feathers)

HYPOTHESIS: The good news is that based on my carefully crafted formula—aka the Drake Equation—the local wood duck population *can* rebound. It's simple math:

$$v + w + x + (y \bullet 2) = z$$

KEY

V = Nesting Box Construction
W = Habitat Restoration
X = Habitat Conservation
Y = Hunting Regulation Enforcement
Z = Local Wood Duck Population Growth

ACTIONS TAKEN: This summer, I helped local volunteers plant new trees in the Santa Rosa wetlands. Wood ducks are "cavity nesters," meaning they like to make homes in small holes where branches fall off trees, so we built and installed twenty-five nesting boxes for the wood ducks up in the existing trees. As a further experiment, I put in one extra box at the waterfall at Noyd Woods Nature Preserve.

CONCLUSION: For now, only time will tell if the Drake Equation is valid!

My project display looked pretty cool. I had a video loop of my group installing nesting boxes in the wetlands, and my display board had photos of me putting up the Noyd Woods nesting box. That location was a long shot, because the waterfall wasn't in the wetlands. In fact, it was really close to where I was getting off the bus right now.

And *that's* why I was excited about hearing a wood duck call. A nesting pair of birds might have moved into the home I'd made for them!

Anyway, as Mr. Berry drove off and the rumble of the bus's engine faded, I scanned the trees below the steep ridge with my eyes. See, wood ducks have gleaming feathers of green, purple, and chestnut brown, so if I spotted a flash of color, then I'd raise my binocs for a closer look.

"Come on," I said. "Where are you?"

"I'm right here," said a familiar voice behind me.

2

WHAT? I WAS SO FOCUSED ON THE DUCK, I HADN'T noticed that someone *else* had gotten off at the bus stop after me.

I turned. And there, grinning and holding a big stick, was a chilling sight: *Coby Cage.*

My stomach dropped like a diving osprey. Remember when I said that I take the bus for my own safety? Coby is who I'm trying to stay safe *from*!

COBY CAGE *(Tyrannus solitaria)*

APPEARANCE: Tall. Lean. A little pigeon-toed.

VOICE: Varies from whispered threats to full-throated calls of anger.

PLUMAGE: Medium-long hair covered by a baseball cap. Likes T-shirts that have to be turned inside out at school because of their antisocial messages.

RANGE: Unpredictable. Able to access wide number of locations by bike, skateboard, or bus.

SOCIAL BEHAVIOR: Can attract large flocks, but prefers being alone. Sometimes seen in company of high school kids. Known to relentlessly pursue a single victim—like me.

STATUS: Endangering.

I know better than to get caught out in the open by Coby. *He's* the reason why I don't walk or ride my bike to school. But Coby's routes are inconsistent. And when he does ride the school bus, it's not always the same one.

Yet I've learned that as long as I take the bus, I get home under the watchful eye of Mr. Berry. So even if Coby's along for the ride, I'm usually okay.

Usually. But now it was just me and him. Alone.

Coby adjusted his baseball cap and grinned. If you saw him and caught the glint of mischief in his eyes, you'd probably think Coby was just an average troublemaker.

But looks are deceiving. Coby is an *above*-average trouble-maker.[2]

Last year, someone hacked into the school's telephone list. Then, during computer lab, that someone sent a one-word text message from the school's official account to all of the parent contacts:

Earthqwake!

The resulting panic was not caused by the message's bad spelling. There were so many phone calls and e-mails to the school, its computer system crashed. Ronnie Ramirez suspects that Coby was the hacker. If he really *was* responsible, our school must have a Gifted and Talented Program in Advanced Pranks. Or maybe Coby was in an after-school program like "Destination Insubordination."

As I stood up there on Pleasant Hill Ridge, he reached out and lightly poked me in the chest with his stick.

Think, I thought, backing up a step. *What would Ronnie do in this situation?* In my best nonargumentative way, I said to Coby, "I see you found a stick."

2. FIELD NOTES: Getting to Know Coby

My first sighting of Coby happened when I was in fifth grade. I was in the hallway, and Coby walked past me.

"What's up, noob?" he asked, snatching the glasses off my face.

A teacher later caught him on the playground using my lenses to set fire to the wood chips under the swings.

Coby laughed. "Tell me something I don't know."

I thought for a second, then replied, "Well, owls can turn their heads almost all the way around, but they can't move their eyes. One local species we have here in Santa Rosa is the short-eared owl. It has zygodactyl feet, which sounds complicated, but it just means that two talons face front and two face back."

Coby was just looking at me blankly, so I took that as a good sign and kept going. "Female short-ears make sort of a barking 'kee-ow' sound, but males have that 'voo-hoo-hoo' call that everyone knows. They migrate, too, but usually at night, so it's not like you're ever going to see a flock of short-eared owls heading south for the winter—" But now Coby was glaring at me. "Wait, did you know all this already?"

"Did *you* know you're the most annoying kid at our school?" asked Coby, shaking his head. Almost to himself, he added, "Man, you totally remind me of *him*." Coby spat out the last word like it tasted bad.

What did I do? And who's this him *who's so annoying?* But I didn't have time to wonder long, because then Coby swung the stick back behind his head like a baseball bat.

"Maybe someone just needs to knock some sense into you," he said angrily.

Uh-oh. My "what would Ronnie do?" strategy had backfired. For an instant, I thought about Fake-Fu, a game I invented with my best friend, Jason. To play, we face off and then start making insane martial arts moves. When it comes to weird face expressions and bogus sound effects, I have a black belt. But could a menacing grimace and *"Hai-bojo-socky!"* battle cry help me now?

Closing my eyes, I pictured a movie scene where I used my Fake-Fu powers to swing my binoculars around and around by their strap, like nunchuks. The scene ends with my binoculars smacking Coby in the head and knocking off his baseball cap.

How great would that be?

I opened my eyes. Coby was still there. His cap was still on.

The stick bobbed back and forth, and as Coby got ready to swing, I got ready to duck. But then he stopped and used the stick to point down the Pleasant Ridge hillside. The ground there dropped steeply for the first hundred feet. In fact, it was more of a cliff than a hill. Then it leveled out into the trees inside the Noyd Woods Nature Preserve.

"I'll give you a choice," said Coby. "If you want to go home, just head that way."

I hesitated. Did I mention I was standing by a cliff?

Swish.

A breeze blew across my face as Coby swung his stick past me. "So what's it gonna be, my fine feathered friend? The stick or the hill?"

I nervously rubbed the scar on my forearm. Looking down

the ridge again, I thought: *If I can keep my speed up, I just might make it—*

Swish.

This time, the stick nicked the end of my nose.

I ran and jumped off the cliff.

3

At first, things went great. I cleared the edge of the embankment, and with a couple of flying leaps, left Coby behind me.

But as I flew downhill, I realized that:

A. The top half of my body was leaning farther and farther forward, so . . .

B. . . . *I couldn't stop.*

After another couple of leaps, I wasn't running downhill anymore. I was *falling* downhill—

"Have a nice *trip*, Noah!" Coby called.

I took another flying leap over a small bush, and then—without warning—an invisible force wrapped itself across my upper chest, belly, and waist. As my downhill velocity pushed me against it, the invisible force pressed back harder and harder.

"URRRK!"

My arms and legs flung forward even as my body was slowing down—and then, for a brief instant, I just hovered in the air, with my eyes wide and my cheeks puffed out!

Oddly, it didn't hurt that much. And I bet, it probably looked pretty awesome, too.

Then the invisible force shot me backward, like a marble in a slingshot. I flew a short distance, and then smashed into the hillside with a *WHUMP*.

Now *that* hurt.

I moaned.

It didn't seem to help.

I groaned.

Still nothing.

Coby called down to me. "Are you okay?" If I hadn't known better, I might have thought he was concerned. "Sorry! Guess you should have looked out for that fence."

Fence? Weakly, I raised my head. *What fence?* And there it was, shining in the sunlight. Three solid wires were strung between sturdy fence posts at the bottom of the hill. But I'd been moving so fast, the wires were invisible until I nose-dived right into them.

And to my right, a sign for something called CATARACT GROVE swung from the wires.

Coby had just chased me into an ambush!

As I lay my head back down, I heard a high, squeaky whistle—was it the wood duck? I listened carefully:

Fwee-feet! Fwee-feet-yeah!

Dang. It wasn't a wood duck's whistle. Probably an American wigeon (*Anas americana*).

"If you're okay, I'm going to take off!" yelled Coby. "Okay?" There was a chuckle, and then that faded and disappeared. Coby's work here was complete—maybe he had his own items to check off his list from the American Troublemakers Association:

☑ Chase *Noahbikulous noobius* down a hill.

Hey, if you'd been there, maybe you'd have laughed, too. That doesn't make you a bad person. After all, I really was flying down the hill with my hands flopping around on my wrists until I hit the wires and got flung back into the dirt.

So have a good laugh. Think about me, just lying there, waiting for the feeling to come back to my legs.

4

At first, I held still and tried to figure out whether I had any broken bones. Next, I wondered what life in a wheelchair was like for my friend Jenny.

And then I got a strange feeling.

I already know what it's like to watch a bird: it's a mix of caution and concentration. But what's it like for the *bird*? Can the bird tell when someone's secretly watching it?

As I lay there, I had an uncanny sense someone was studying *me*. But who? I turned my head to look around, and as I did, stars glittered at the edge of my vision. *Great*, I thought. *So I'm all dirty,* and *I have a concussion.*

But the stars weren't floating around, like when Jason "accidentally" kicked a soccer ball off my head. When I looked directly at them, these stars didn't dance away. Instead, they twinkled from just one spot. There, half-hidden beneath the bush I'd jumped over, was a bright . . . *something*.

I squinted and made out a round disc reflecting sunlight. *What is that?* I crawled closer and reached for it. That feeling of being watched grew stronger. Picking up the glinting disc, I felt a warm, smooth surface. Somehow it glittered green and purple at once, depending on the angle I looked at it.

It's iridescent. I held it in my hand, my fingers slipping easily into the five indents around the disc's edge. I gently tried to squeeze the pancake-size thing. It bent and flexed a little, but then stiffened like it was made of hard plastic.

Now this will sound weird, but as I did this, I could have sworn I felt something bend and flex inside of me too. It was the oddest feeling—as if my body was shifting from one thing to another, like that moment when you think you're going to sneeze but haven't sneezed yet.

And then the feeling passed.

I shrugged and turned the disc over. It had a slight bulge on the side, but that was about it. *Is this a toy?* I wondered. *Maybe it's jewelry? Or a Frisbee for a rich leprechaun?*

One more thing—as soon as I picked the disc up, the sense that someone was watching me intensified. I looked around again warily—but nope, I really was all alone. Just a dirt-covered kid hanging out with his new friends—a bush and a sparkly pancake.

Between the creepy feeling of being watched and Coby's ambush, this seemed like a good time to be extra careful. I didn't want to borrow trouble, and so I went to put the sparkling disc back where I'd found it . . . when a small black bird zipped overhead.

Was that what I think it was?

Suddenly nothing else mattered.

Shoving the sparkly pancake in my cargo shorts, I scrambled to my feet and spied the black bird heading for the trees at Noyd Falls.

Coby Cage, my hurt back, even the wood duck—all of it was instantly forgotten. A new hunt was on. I ducked under the fence and ran like a maniac into the woods.

* * *

Noyd Nature Preserve is inside Santa Rosa's city limits. At almost one thousand acres, it's a small wilderness—and it's almost right outside my front door. This is lucky for me, because lots and *lots* of birds live there or migrate through it: chickadees, creepers, owls, finches, swallows, jays, hawks, grosbeaks, tanagers, vultures, woodpeckers, warblers . . .

After we moved to Santa Rosa, I got to know all of the preserve's dirt trails pretty fast. One trail goes right through a small grove of giant, silent redwoods; another winds through oak woodlands and thorny thickets of wild blackberry, then pops out into a meadow that blooms with orange poppies in the spring.

A creek also runs through the preserve year-round, and it actually cascades right off a cliff. Cool, right? That's Noyd Falls.

It drops about twenty feet through the air into a small, circular canyon. Over the years, Noyd Falls has carved out its own pool of water. And *this* was where I was hoping to spot my mystery bird.

Have you ever gone bird-watching before? If not, you'd never believe how exciting it is. Some people say birding is like hunting, but without any blood. Whatever. All I know is that birders need to look all around, from the ground to the skies, trying to notice *everything* around them.

When you're totally aware like that, your heart starts beating fast. But you need to stay calm! And if you see the bird that you're looking for? That thrill is just about the greatest feeling around.

So now you know how excited I was when I got to Noyd Falls. Its pool was surrounded by ferns and protected from the sun by trees, and it was a relief to feel the heat dip. There was a *snap* as a dead branch gave way under my foot. But luckily, the splashing water covered the noise.

I hid behind a maple tree and looked around. From where I was standing, I could see the front of the wood duck nesting box that I'd stuck up in a nearby tree last year. But it showed no signs of being lived in by ducks or anything else.

Next I turned my hopeful eyes to the waterfall. Behind the cascade, mossy wet rock ledges stretched left and right.

And *that's* where my eyes glimpsed movement! But I needed a closer look. So slowly, I brought my binoculars up. . . .

And there it was—the same bird that I'd seen flying. It was small, with a dark back pattern, and was flattened against the rocks. Amazingly, the bird was nimbly crawling sideways *toward* the cascading water. As it crawled, it kept its head turned to the side. That way, it could keep one eye on the canyon.

This was one sly bird.

Bird-watchers are patient, so even though my blood was racing, I held perfectly still. Through my lenses, I could see the bird's rounded gray head, with its big eyes and small beak. Black patches around the bird's eyes made it look like a bandit.

But what kind of bird *was* it? I couldn't be sure yet, but I had a wild theory. One of the most mysterious birds in North America is the black swift, and it's really hard to spot. For one thing, the black swift is usually silent, so there's no birdsong to give it away.

Even trickier, the black swift often nests *behind* waterfalls. Can you believe it? A nest of moss on a cold, wet rock with water spraying all around is its idea of home!

I didn't want to take my eyes off the bird, but I needed more info. As the splashing water echoed off the rock walls, I carefully reached down into my backpack and pulled out a copy of *An Informal Pocket Guide to Western Birds*. My hands shook a little as I flipped through the pages—and there it was:

*Known for its secretive lifestyle, the **black swift** flies so fast and so high, it has been called "the cloud dweller." It spends* *most waking hours in flight, catching insects in midair. Though its travel paths are generally unknown, the birds have been tracked between United States and Brazil, a round-trip of 8,600 miles.*

Status: Total population may not exceed about 15,000 birds. Even so, wildlife experts don't know if the black swift should be listed as "endangered" or simply "mystifying." Forest destruction and water shortages in the United States and the clearing of the Amazon in Brazil pose clear dangers. Further, the female only lays one egg at a time, so the bird's reproductive rate is low even under ideal circumstances.

Voice: The black swift rarely sings. Even a hungry baby black swift will usually stay quiet. However, when an adult nears its nest, a hungry chick will often make a surprisingly deep plik-plik-plik-plik *sound. . . .*

And right then I heard it, almost lost in the splashing of Noyd Falls.

Plik-plik-plik-plik.

NO WAY. I was so excited, I must have moved, because the little bird cocked its gray head to the side. Suddenly the black swift hopped off the rock, zipped into the air, and disappeared like an arrow shot from a bow.

As it flew off, I almost high-fived myself. I knew, I mean I just *knew*, that I was the only person to have seen this! And if

I could confirm the sighting? The black swift would be my biggest bird-watching score ever!

I imagined the glory of marking my checklist.

☑ Black swift *(Cypseloides niger)*

A thrill swept from my scalp to my toes (even my right big toe, which was sticking through a hole in my sock). Goose bumps covered my arms. I had to tell someone—*anyone*—about this right away.

And so another domino fell. How was I supposed to know that such a little bird would lead to such BIG trouble?

5

PICKING UP THE TRAIL OUT OF NOYD WOODS, I RAN down into my neighborhood, heading straight for Jason's house. Well, *almost* straight—I had to detour across the street to get around a huge truck with a crane that was blocking the sidewalk. And as I crossed, I almost got run over by a flock of young kids on bikes. *Sheesh! Kids.*

One of them, a girl with streamers on her handlebars, turned to stare at me as she went past. And none of them said "Sorry!" or anything. As I watched the little menaces go off, I noticed something. They were all practically pedaling in unison. If they had been birds, their wings would have been flapping in perfect rhythm.

Anyway, I knocked on Jason's front door and my best friend answered, then stepped back in surprise. "Wow, what happened to *you*, Pigpen? Come in and wash your face, then we can chill."

JASON BRIGHT *(Bene-vestitum athleta)*

APPEARANCE: Strong build. Black hair. Blue eyes.

VOICE: Talks fast, often about himself.

PLUMAGE: Favors sportswear; especially likes colorful soccer jerseys and (in winter months) tracksuits.

RANGE: Found on basketball courts and soccer fields.

SOCIAL BEHAVIOR: Has a friendly, outgoing personality. Opinionated; sometimes takes a joke too far.

STATUS: Semipopular.

As I cleaned up, I filled Jason in on my adventures—the bus ride, Coby, the weird object I'd found, and of course, the black swift. By the time I finished talking, we'd ended up in his room. It was hot and stuffy there, even with the window open. *So much for chilling.*

"Why does Coby hate you so much, anyway?" Jason was lying on his bed, adjusting the straps of a colorfully spattered paintball helmet.

"I don't know!" I said. "That guy's been out to get me ever since I moved here."

"He's definitely got issues, but still—there must be a reason," said Jason. "Anyway, it's cool that you found that duck."

"No," I said. "You're not listening. It's not a duck. I think I found a *black swift*." I waited a second to let the huge importance of that seep in.

Jason kept playing with his helmet.

"They're really rare," I added. "And they live behind waterfalls. Did you know—"

"Hey, if *you* care about a little bird, then *I* care." Jason brushed at the front of his brilliant-blue soccer shirt. "Anyway, let's see that leprechaun Frisbee you found."

I handed Jason the thick sparkly pancake I'd spotted under the bush. "I have no idea what this thing is."

Jason turned the disc over in his hands. "Looks like someone covered a hockey puck in glitter," he muttered. "Then they flattened it with a steamroller."

"Huh," I grunted, looking out the window.

The Brights' neighbor, Mrs. Damaschino, ran a day care. I could hear the children shouting loudly next door—and for little kids, they sure made a lot of noise. In Jason's backyard, a lawn sprinkler spun lazily, spraying onto the Brights' new swimming pool. And there was Jason's dad, pulling the sprinkler to a new spot.

I was happy to see Mr. Bright. After all, he's one of my favorite grown-ups ever.

MR. THOMAS BRIGHT *(Parrotus widowus)*

APPEARANCE: Burly male with more hair on his arms than most humans have on their heads.

VOICE: ALWAYS YELLS, EVEN WHEN WHISPERING.

PLUMAGE: Wears colorful Hawaiian shirts (yet has never been to Hawaii).

RANGE: Like all adults, he can drive great distances. (Yet, as noted, he is not found in Hawaii.)

SOCIAL BEHAVIOR: Aggressively friendly.

STATUS: Mated for life; now finds himself a single parent.

Shading his eyes against the sun, Mr. Bright looked back at me. "HELLO, NOAH!" he yelled.

"Hi, Mr. Bright," I called from the window.

"SEE IF YOU CAN GET JASON TO CLEAN UP THAT WASTELAND HE CALLS A BEDROOM," Mr. Bright said. "AND PLEASE ASK HIM TO HELP HIS SISTER WITH THE LAUNDRY."

Giving Mr. Bright a thumbs-up, I turned back to Jason. To

my surprise, his face was now lit by a bright-green glow coming from—the pancake?

"Hey! What did you do?"

Jason shrugged, turning the disc around so I could see. "I just pressed this little knob on the side and a blank screen opened up."

I took it from him. Sure enough, an egg-shaped screen now filled one side of the disc. But it *wasn't* blank—the screen was lit with a green background, and in the center was a round icon like a ball. Underneath that was a single word:

ADEPTNESS

The ball pulsed slightly.

I pushed the pancake's stem experimentally, and the oval screen disappeared. I mean, it didn't slide out of view—instead, it was just instantly *gone*. I ran my finger over the disc's surface where the screen had been. Nothing. It was perfectly smooth.

I pressed the stem again and the screen blinked right back into view, as if it had been there all along.

"That's weird."

"Hey, maybe it's like a squished Magic 8 Ball," Jason said. "Try shaking it, and we can ask it a question."

I shook it up and down. "Ask away," I said.

"Will I win my soccer game this weekend?"

I stopped shaking, pressed the knob, and pretended to read

from the puck's screen: "ALL SIGNS POINT TO NO," I said, "BECAUSE YOU SUCK."

Before Jason could make a comeback, there was a *crunch* at the door. Jenny had crushed some potato chips on Jason's floor as she rolled into the room in her wheelchair. She had a pile of clean beach towels on her lap and a look of disgust on her face.

"Jason, this room is a total health hazard," she said.

JENNY BRIGHT *(Fortis bellator)*

APPEARANCE: Jenny has strong shoulders and pale-blue eyes, like her brother.

VOICE: Despite young age, can have the tone of a teacher, parent, or other authority figure.

PLUMAGE: Jenny's hair is naturally black but is currently dyed pink and orange. (And last week? Purple.)

RANGE/SOCIAL BEHAVIOR: Range somewhat limited by wheelchair. Caring personality, very self-confident. Can sometimes verge on bossy.

STATUS: Popular-ish, though less outgoing since the accident.

It was true. Every drawer of Jason's dresser was open and empty. Science-fiction books carpeted the carpet. Empty hangers hung in his closet. Below them were piles of T-shirts, shoes, shorts, and dumbbells. These piles flowed out of the closet and into the room, where charging cords snaked in and out of them.

It hadn't always been this way. A couple of years ago, Jason's bedroom was just an average mess. But after the accident, Jason just kind of stopped putting his stuff away. It was like he was *done* with that.

The odd thing is that Jason is a total neat freak about his looks. His hair and his clothes have to be perfect before he'll go out. Jason's room even has a full-length mirror where he can preen and admire himself.

I glanced in that mirror and checked myself out.

NOAH GROW *(Avis custo maximus)*

APPEARANCE: Peanut-butter-colored hair, big ears, lots of teeth. My parents say I'm "built like a reed," whatever that means.

VOICE: Medium pitch, nasal. Vocal speed picks up when excited.

PLUMAGE: Wears glasses. Typically seen in faded shorts and old T-shirts that blend well into the background. (Bright clothes scare birds away.)

RANGE: Can be found in areas near home accessible by foot or bike. Sometimes migrates much farther in the summer, depending on parents' work projects.

SOCIAL BEHAVIOR: Sometimes seen with friends, but often alone, observing warm-blooded, egg-laying, feathered vertebrates.

STATUS: Invisible-ish.

Meanwhile, Jason was arguing with his sister. "A health hazard? Please. My room is totally organized." He pointed at the floor. "Look, the clothes are with the clothes."

Jenny pointed to some small red objects. "And what are *those*?"

Leaning forward, Jason grinned. "I think those are goji berries."

"That does it," said Jenny. She grabbed the pile of warm towels off her lap and threw them on top of her brother. "You heard Dad—fold those towels."

Like her brother, Jenny's my friend, too. Because even though she and Jason are opposites, they're also inseparable. With the twins, everything's a package deal.

"Wow, Noah," Jenny said, finally noticing my dirty clothes. "I'm not even going to *ask* what happened to you. Want to play some air hockey later?"

This was a bad offer to accept. Jenny's the best air hockey player ever. True, she doesn't have much of a reach from her wheelchair, but she makes up for it with hawklike reflexes.

Before I could answer, she spotted the iridescent purple green disc in my hand. "What's that?" Jenny moved forward with a *SQUISH*. (Those were the goji berries.)

Before I could explain, she took the puck from my hand and peered at its screen. "Dead batteries," she said dismissively, tossing it onto Jason's bed.

But I could *see* that the disc's green screen was still brightly lit. To check, I reached over and tapped the pulsing ball icon. And a list of options dropped down. "It's not dead at all." I held the glittering disc up for Jenny to see. "Check out the pull-down menu."

Jenny squinted at the screen. "*Right,*" she scoffed. "It must be a 'pulling-my-leg menu,' because *nothing's* there. Seriously, what *is* that thing, anyway?"

"Noah's been busy," said Jason. He'd escaped from the pile of towels and was folding them into stacks. "Since school got out, he's discovered a magic puck *and* a new kind of bird."

"I didn't *discover* a bird. I just spotted one that might be really important," I argued. "And this isn't my puck—I found it in Noyd Woods. Someone must have lost it."

Jenny pursed her lips. "Well, if that thing's lost, and *if* you can really read its menu, then look up ice."

"And how is frozen water going to help?" I asked.

Jenny and Jason smiled at each other. Their smile said *We know something you don't know.*

I hate that smile.

"You'd know," scolded Jenny, "if your parents would just break down and get you a cell phone."

"Yeah," added Jason. "Take a break from the birds and learn about *our* species. We humans know that 'ice' stands for In Case of Emergency."

Oh!

This sort of thing happened all the time. Although the twins complain about it, I think they like explaining things like this to me. After all, everyone wants to feel like an expert about something, right?

"That thing's owner might've listed her contact info there," said Jenny. "So, all you have to do is choose ICE on the menu. If it gives you an e-mail or phone number, just tell the person that you've got her . . . sparkly thing."

I looked down at the purple-green puck and tapped the ball icon. The menu dropped down again, but it was totally confusing—just a jumble of words, and even as I read them, some words disappeared while new ones slid into their place. But at least they seemed to be listed alphabetically.

"So, Noah, unless you're faking your magical ability to read the screen," instructed Jenny, "just go to the letter *I*."

Scrolling, I saw she was right. There it was: ICE.

"Got it!" I said. "I'll check it later."

"Don't be such a chicken, Noah," said Jason. "Do it now. I mean, there might be a reward!"

Jenny smiled. "Yeah, you wouldn't want to do the right thing unless money was involved."

I looked at the purple-green puck glittering in my hand. What I *really* wanted to do was get home and report my black swift sighting to the U.S. Fish and Wildlife Service. But it's hard to say no to the twins—so I almost never do.

Still, I hesitated as I held my thumb over the oval screen. *This doesn't feel right.* I remembered how I'd felt someone was watching me in the nature preserve. And I remembered how I'd wanted to just leave this thing where I found it.

"Do it!" urged Jason.

"And stop slouching," added Jenny.

Fine. Throwing my shoulders back, I pressed ICE. Nothing. I tried tapping the stem on the side. That did it—now my selection was blinking on the screen:

ICE

ICE

ICE

And another domino fell.

6

"I DON'T REALLY GET WHAT IT'S DOING," I SAID, showing the puck's flashing screen to the twins.

"It's not *doing* anything," said Jason. "It's blank."

"Why are you being so weird?" asked Jenny.

Confused, I double-checked the screen.

ICE

ICE

ICE

It WAS flashing.

Scratching the scar on my arm, I glanced out at the backyard sprinkler. I was trying to do a good deed, but I just didn't like talking on the phone much, even with friends. And even if I did get hold of this thing's owner, what would I say?

"Hi, did you lose a squished puck covered in glitter? You know, a thing shaped like a pancake with a secret screen that only some people can read? If you did, then I found it. The puck, I mean. Under a bush."

Awk-ward. I looked at the twins and shrugged—and as I did, the iridescent puck vibrated slightly in my hand.

Is it my imagination, I wondered, or is this thing cooling off?

"What is it?" asked Jenny. She'd noticed my flinch.

It wasn't my imagination—the purple-green puck was getting cold. It was SO cold, my hand was cold, too. Really cold. A chill radiated from the disc to my hand—and then it raced up my forearm. The cold took the turn at my elbow fast, and leaped up my upper arm to my shoulder.

I yelped and jumped to my feet. From my shoulder, icicles crept into my chest—and now an icy finger was reaching up my neck, stabbing deep inside my skull! The frosty feeling spread fast, into my mouth and face.

I tried to speak, but my tongue was thick and my teeth were aching, like I'd eaten way too much ice cream, way too fast. All I got out was "Datz COLD."

"Dude, what IS it?" asked Jason.

I tried to speak clearly. "Hrain hreeze."

The twins stared at me like I'd lost my mind.

"Hrain hreeze!" I shouted, pointing at my head.

What is going on? I tried to calm down. Everyone knows that brain freezes always go away. Just relax and think warm *thoughts,* I told myself. I gazed out the window and focused on the hot sun sparkling off the pool's water—

I began to shiver and shake. I was FREEZING.

"Something's wrong," Jenny said. "Noah, let go of that thing!"

I tried to open my hand to drop the puck, but it was too late—my fingers were frozen shut around it. All I could do was mindlessly shake my hand up and down.

Jason stepped forward and grabbed my hand.

"Whoa, he IS frozen!" My friend pried my fingers apart, and the purple-green puck fell to the bed. Jenny spun around, grabbed it, and juggled the disc like a hot potato—or a really cold one.

"How do I hang up?" she squeaked. "I pushed the little knob on the side and the screen closed. Did that help?"

NO!

Desperate for warmth, I grabbed a striped towel off the warm laundry on the bed. Quickly I wrapped it around my head; Jason pulled a puffy down jacket from his closet floor and threw it over my shoulders.

Jenny pointed out the window. "Noah, go outside to warm up!"

Good idea! Lunging out of Jason's bedroom, I ran down the hall and outside to the backyard patio.

A war was waging inside my body—I was deeply chilled, but I was so panicked, my body was sweating. As I stood there, in a cold sweat on the hot bricks, a large green ball floated over the fence and splashed in the Brights' swimming pool.

"I'll get it!" rang out a chorus of high voices, followed by scrabbling sounds. Then tiny hands began popping up on top of the fence.

The preschoolers were fearlessly storming the yard to get their ball back. But before the assault could work, the little hands started disappearing. Mrs. Damaschino must have been plucking them off the fence, one after another.

Meanwhile, I tried taking some deep breaths. Despite the sunshine, the jacket, and the beach towel on my head, I wasn't thawing out—instead, the brain freeze was reaching deeper into my chest and moving down my belly and into my other arm. Looking at my scar, I saw the sweat on my skin turn into tiny ice crystals.

Jenny and Jason appeared on either side of me. "Try to relax," said Jenny, as if she were babysitting me. "Just chill out."

I tried to say "That's the LAST thing I should do!" But all that came out was a frozen croak: "*Dazdastingdoodoo!*"

"He's delirious!" cried Jason.

Now the brain freeze had sunk to my waist.

What if I get butt freeze? I thought. *I'll DIE.* My fear built to a breaking point, and I raised my cold hands to my freezing face.

"Is there any way you can just . . . let it out?" exhorted Jason.

I was willing to try anything. I pointed my freezing fists at the green ball floating in the swimming pool. And I watched as a blue-white bolt of *something* poured out of my fists—

CLINK!

We all froze.

I mean, nobody moved.

Jenny and Jason looked at each other, their mouths making round Os. As for me, although my shocked brain barely registered it, I could already feel warmth returning to my body.

I unwrapped the beach towel from my head while Jenny moved over to the pool. She looked at the green ball. It wasn't bobbing up and down anymore. Jenny frowned and looked at the water. She eased over to the ramp that she used to get into the swimming pool and reached down to touch the water's surface with her knuckles.

Tap, tap, tap.

Jenny looked back at me.

"Noah," she said, "you just froze our pool."

"What?" I said. "Very funny." But the green ball still hadn't moved.

Jason walked over. Gingerly, he put his toe on the surface of the water. Then his foot.

Then his *other* foot.

The pool held Jason's weight. He stepped out onto the pool, turned on the ice, and looked at me with wide eyes.

"You froze our pool," Jason whispered unbelievingly. He

hopped a little on the ice and looked down. "You froze our pool *solid*." He looked up. "How'd you do that?"

"I'm really sorry," I said. "Am I in trouble?"

"Are you kidding?" Jenny rolled over to me and grinned. "This is the greatest day of my life!"

7

THE THREE OF US STARED FEARFULLY AT THE PUCK.
It lay where I'd dropped it on Jason's bed, glittering innocently
next to his paintball helmet.

I was warmer now, but I still shivered just looking at it.
"What. Just. Happened?"

"You messed around with that . . . thing," said Jenny, ticking off the events on her fingers. "You freaked out. And you
wrapped your head in a towel and ran outside yelling."

"And *then*," continued Jason, "you froze our swimming pool."

Jenny gave a little shrug. "But other than that, I didn't see
anything weird."

We all laughed and sounded a little hysterical.

I shrugged off Jason's down jacket while Jenny gingerly
picked the purple-green puck up from the bed. "It's so small,"
she said. "Did we just dream that whole thing?"

On cue, we all looked out the window. The frozen surface of

the pool was already melting in the heat. And as we watched, a small iceberg surfaced, gently spun in the sunshine, and fell over with a splash.

"I guess not." I pointed at the puck. "But how? Why? What *is* that thing?" (I almost added *Could it be magic?* but thought better of it.)

Jenny carefully set the purple-green disc back down. "It must be from a tech company or something. Like somehow this prototype from the research department got lost, and then you found it."

"Lost in the middle of the woods?" asked Jason skeptically. "More likely that thing was *planted* there. And I'll bet it wasn't a tech company that did that, but some reality show. I mean, please, someone must be pranking us." He slyly looked out the window. "Noah, their cameras are probably out there right now. C'mon, let's see if you can get that puck to work again!"

Is he serious?

"You might have missed it, Jason, but I almost *froze* to death just now! Whatever that thing is and wherever it came from, it's dangerous. Very dangerous."

But Jason wasn't convinced. "Look, we already have flame-throwers that shoot flames. What's such a big deal about something that shoots ice?"

"Jason," I said, my voice rising, "did you miss the part where the ice came out of my HANDS?"

He nodded grudgingly. "Good point."

Jenny turned around to look at me. "Look, Noah, we got caught by surprise that time. But now we know what to expect. Plus, this thing might be able to do other, safer things."

I couldn't believe my still-chilly ears. "Thumbs-down. Why aren't you guys more freaked-out by this?"

"Um, because it's cool?!" Jason looked surprised, then grinned. "Hey, I made a joke and wasn't even trying!"

"What if our science teacher, Mrs. Sanchez, were here?" coaxed Jenny. "I'll bet you'd agree with what she said. After all, you worship the ground she walks on."

"You're exaggerating," I said. "I just *like* it."

Jason moved a foam football off the chair by his desk and sat down. "Well, when you marry Mrs. Sanchez, don't forget to invite me."

"How could I? You're going to be the Worst Man."

Jason gave me an appreciative nod. "Nice one! Well, I'll bet Mrs. Sanchez would say we should run a controlled experiment." He swiveled in the chair and glanced at Jenny, as if they were a tag team.

"And what about Anemona?" Jenny asked. "I bet if your favorite little airhead—I mean, *redhead*—asked, you'd experiment with the puck in a heartbeat."

I glared at her. Jenny knew my weak spot, and her name is as unique as the girl herself—Anemona Hartliss.

How can I describe Anemona? Just think of the best-looking, most popular girl at your school. Now imagine her *better*.

ANEMONA HARTLISS *(Gorgias magnificens)*

APPEARANCE: Stunning.

VOICE: Clear, and silvery.

SMELL: Anemona leaves behind the scent of lilacs. (Or honeysuckle. Whatever.)

PLUMAGE: Emerald-green eyes. Soft red hair the color of autumn leaves.

RANGE: Found in classrooms and at the popular table at lunch. Impulsive behavior can sometimes lead to odd locations. (Ex.: In fifth grade P.E., Anemona shimmied up a column and waved hello to the teacher from the gym's roof.) After school, patterns are mysterious.

SOCIAL BEHAVIOR: Will flock with large groups, but also known to be a free bird.

SIMILAR SPECIES: None.

STATUS: Not endangered, but one-of-a-kind.

Last year, I learned a bitter lesson in our school cafetorium. (You know, the cafeteria/auditorium?) That was where I made the mistake of telling Jason about my crush on Anemona.[3] See, Jason was talking about his two favorite topics: soccer and himself. "So that header was my second goal of the match. . . ."

But *my* attention was on Anemona. There she was, three tables over, with her mega-popular friends, Mindy Grimsley and Beth Partridge. As I watched, Mindy said something funny, and Anemona laughed, tossing back her mane of flaming-red hair.

My heart twinged. *What if I could make Anemona laugh like that? Would she toss her hair for me?*

Jason's eyes followed my gaze. "Oh, *I* see what's going on here," he said. "So, even people from your planet have feelings, huh?"

"What?" I said innocently. I tried to keep my face expressionless—no way did I want Jason knowing about this.

"I have to admit you have good taste," said Jason. "Mindy is super cute." And then he looked over at the girls' table—and waved. Mindy and Beth both looked over. And to my horror, Jason *kept* waving.

"Jason," I hissed. "Stop that!"

---

3. FIELD NOTES: The Lure of Anemona
    I've had a secret crush on Anemona since we were in the same art class in sixth grade. On our first day, the teacher, Mr. Sandwick, asked Anemona about her name during roll call.
    "It's Greek," Anemona answered with a flip of her hair. "It means 'daughter of the wind.'"
    Wow, I thought. *How cool is that?* (Then I accidentally knocked my colored markers off the desk.)

Mindy was drinking from a straw. As she spotted Jason, she looked like she wanted to blow a poison dart out of her straw and into his neck. Then she and Beth made barfing faces and turned their attention back to Anemona. As for Jason, he wasn't discouraged. "Did you see Mindy? Sorry, Noah, but your girlfriend just fell in love with me," he said. "But Mindy doesn't want to face it yet, so I'm going to give her a little time."

To keep Jason on the wrong track, I played along. "Yeah, I can tell Mindy has feelings for you," I said sincerely. "Feelings of hate and disgust."

And then Anemona stood, and my eyes were drawn to her like magnets. Again, Jason caught me looking.

"Wait, you like *Anemona*?" he exclaimed. "I'm impressed. Way to set your sights high, son. Also? You're nuts."

I gave a sad sigh. See, I was old enough then to know the way of the world—nobody likes the person who likes them. But I couldn't deny my feelings anymore. "Okay, Jason, you're right. But you have to *swear* not to tell anyone!"

"Don't worry, Noah. Trust me; I'll keep your secret safe." Jason tore his eyes away from Mindy. "Now where was I? Oh, next the referee gave me a yellow card for arguing calls—"

The next day, at the start of English class, Jenny came over to my desk. "I wonder if Anemona likes bird-watching?" she said innocently.

I blushed furiously.

I mean, I blushed *and* I was furious.

"I think she might be kind of into it," added Jenny, now smirking.

Did you see how long Jason lasted with my secret? Not even *one* day.

But we all have our weaknesses. For example, Superman's strength is weakened by kryptonite. And Jason's ability to keep a secret is weakened by anyone who talks to him.

* * *

As the Brights' swimming pool melted, I knew Jenny was just name-checking Anemona to get me to use the iridescent puck again.

"No way I'm touching that thing," I insisted, sticking my hands under my armpits to warm them up.

"Look, you're still cold!" Jenny said. "There must be some of that 'freezing energy' stuck inside you. So I've got an idea. And for it, all we have to do is go into the kitchen. You won't even have to *touch* that . . ." She pointed at the glittering disc. "Wait, what do we call this thing?"

I shrugged. "The puck?"

"Fine," said Jenny, gesturing to the door. "Shall we?"

Now here's the thing—like her brother, Jenny also went through a big change after the accident two years ago. Going from an active lifestyle to a wheelchair was part of it. But while Jenny grew more private about some things, she also spoke her mind more. A lot more. And now what Jenny says goes.

Plus, my thawing brain couldn't think of an argument against her plan. So I reluctantly nodded. Jason whooped happily and ran out, with Jenny right behind. I grabbed another towel from the laundry pile and followed.

In the kitchen, Jenny had Jason fill a glass pitcher at the sink. "Here's the idea. Jason pours out the water into the sink, and you see if you can sort of . . . *aim* at it."

Since the plan didn't involve the purple-green puck, it seemed like a decent idea. But how to get ready? I touched the scar on my arm (it's a nervous habit, okay?), and then stretched my arms over my head. After that, I bent over and tried to touch my toes.

Finally, I shook out my arms and my fingers the way Olympic swimmers do before a race.

"Noah, what are you doing?" asked Jason.

"Just getting ready," I answered, twisting my head around and from side to side.

Jenny rolled her eyes. "Can you not be weird for like two minutes? Let's go!"

"Hang on." Just in case I got brain freeze again, I wrapped the towel carefully around my head. Then I stuck my fists forward and nodded grimly to Jason. "Okay. I'm ready."

"You look great," Jason said with a straight face. Then he started slowly pouring water from the pitcher into the sink. As the water splashed, I tried to force the coldness inside of me out through my knuckles.

A few moments later, the last of the pitcher's water swirled down the drain.

Nothing had happened.

"Well, *that* was exciting," said Jason, as I stared at my knuckles in disappointment.

Jenny looked thoughtful. "Maybe we just need something to get the snowball rolling." She opened up the freezer. A second later, she slipped an ice cube into my left hand. "Hold the ice in one hand and try pointing your other hand at the water."

Ninety minutes ago, I was getting off the school bus. An hour ago, I saw a bird that might be a black swift. And now I'm standing in a kitchen, trying to shoot ice from my hands?

Jason refilled the pitcher while I squeezed the wet ice cube in my left hand and closed my eyes. Then I tried to channel the ice cube's cold sensation across my body and through my right finger.

"Here goes," I said. I could hear Jason pouring water into the sink, so I raised my right hand and pointed a finger in his direction.

"Remember," Jason warned, "don't hit *me.*"

"Don't worry," I said, opening my eyes. "I don't think—"

But seeing the pouring water triggered something inside me. It was as if someone had turned on a hose. I felt a small wave of cold leave the ice cube in my hand, go up my left arm, and then cross my chest (*brrrr*) down my right arm and to my hand.

A thin ray of blue-white energy shot out the end of my finger. Luckily, I was still aiming, and as the ray hit the water pouring from the pitcher there was a—

crackle.

Surprised, I dropped the ice cube. My finger immediately "turned off," and I held it up to my face to inspect it.

It still looked like a finger.

Meanwhile, Jason reached into the sink and pulled out a handful of what looked like shaved ice.

"It worked," said Jenny incredulously. "It worked!"

The three of us held still and looked at one another. Something BIG was happening here. *But what?*

"HEY, YOU KIDS!"

We flinched.

"CAN SOMEONE EXPLAIN TO ME WHY THERE ARE *ICEBERGS* IN OUR SWIMMING POOL?"

8

BUSTED!

I must have looked panicked, because Jenny quietly reassured me. "Don't worry, I got this." Then she yelled back to her father at the top of her lungs. "We're doing a science experiment for school!"

There was quiet, and then some grumbling in the distance (". . . DIDN'T HAVE TO FREEZE THE POOL WHEN I WAS YOUR AGE . . ."), but it slowly trailed off.

"That excuse works every time," Jenny said. Meanwhile, Jason ran out of the kitchen, and I looked out the window and watched a familiar group of younger kids pedal slowly past the house. One of them, a plump boy on a bright-orange bike, was pointing energetically at the crane and the power pole. But before I could wonder what they were up to, Jason ran back in with the puck and set it on the kitchen counter.

I shivered.

"Hey, Noah, just look at this thing's menu again," said Jason. "It might give us some clues."

I didn't move.

"Come *on*," Jenny said. "We'd do it, but neither Jason or I can even *read* it. Think of this as a mystery. I mean, who knows what else your puck can do."

"Maybe you could use it to *fly*," suggested Jason helpfully. "That'd be handy for watching, you know, ducks and stuff."

I shook my head. "Why don't I just put it back where I found it?"

Jason was having none of that. "Listen, I'm the guy who pried that puck from your cold, living fingers. And *I* say—"

Just then, a dull crack and loud shouts from outside cut off his argument. Jason and I jostled each other rushing to the front window. To our left, we could see some of the preschoolers playing in a lawn sprinkler on Mrs. Damaschino's front lawn. In front of us, we could see a minivan backing up fast on the street. It veered over the sidewalk—

"Whoa!" I cried, as Jenny came up beside me. After all, it was an out-of-control driver who had swerved onto a sidewalk and put her in that wheelchair.

The three of us stared as the minivan backed *over* the fire hydrant in the Brights' lawn strip. With a *WHOOSH*, a geyser of water erupted as the hydrant rolled into the gutter.

Then the minivan let loose with an unending *HOOOOONK*. It pulled slightly forward, and a man got out and took off running, leaving the honking car behind.

"What's he *doing*?" I yelled.

Jenny pointed to the right. "He's trying to get away from THAT!"

I looked over to where the truck with the crane was parked next to a telephone pole. Its cherry picker was extended up, and a worker in an orange vest was in its nest, feverishly pushing buttons on its control panel.

The worker didn't care about the broken fire hydrant. That's because he was distracted by the broken telephone pole next to him! It had snapped halfway up, and the falling pole had smashed into the top of his truck. It was balanced there, looming at an angle over the street, like a sparking teeter-totter. But instead of falling the rest of the way down, the pole was caught and held in place by its power lines.

The minivan's honking got even louder as Jason and I ran out of the house and down to the front yard. And from next door, the preschool kids in the sprinkler had run down to the sidewalk. Mrs. Damaschino was outside, trying to stop more children from pouring out of her front door. But one little boy kept laughing and running just out of her reach. I saw her disappear around the corner of her house, chasing after him.

As for the other kids, a couple gawked at the wrecked car and the phone pole. But with Mrs. Damaschino out of the picture, they ran down to the fire hydrant. Its fountain was making a pool by the curb, and the kids were yelling and splashing in it.

Jason said something, but I couldn't hear over the shouting kids, the roaring water, and the minivan's *HOOOOONK.*

"*What?*"

"Those kids are amazing!" Jason said admiringly. "You'd think they'd just gotten to Disneyland."

I tugged his sleeve. "We should go call nine-one-one."

But Jason shook his head and pointed in front of the crane. Three older kids on bikes had stopped there. Two had their smartphones out, so it seemed pretty obvious they were making the emergency call.

But after a second, I saw they were actually taking *photos.* Then one kid said something, and another one laughed.

Who cracks jokes at a disaster?

I peered at the three figures, squinting. The one in the front had on a black baseball cap. I knew that hat. It belonged to Coby Cage.

A respectful distance behind Coby and his pals, the small flock of younger kids on bikes had gathered. The girl with streamers on her handlebars pointed and started to pedal closer. But then the kid on the bright-orange bike held out his arm and waved the group back.

Jason leaned in close to my ear. "Nothing like a disaster to bring a neighborhood together!"

The man in the crane had spotted us. "HEY, MY CONTROLS AREN'T WORKING! GO GET—"

A loud *crack* cut him off as the wires on one side of the pole gave way. A split second later, the power pole came all the way down, trailing broken lines behind it—

Whump!

The power pole hit the street and bounced, shooting sparks all the way to where we stood. And amazingly, the little kids in the hydrant pool started cheering.

At the same time, Mr. Bright sprinted past us, down the driveway. He spotted us, and bellowed, "GET THOSE KIDS OUT OF THERE!" He was pointing excitedly at something, something in the street—

I followed the line of his finger and saw that the pool of water by the gushing fire hydrant was growing—and getting closer to the fallen power pole.

That pool of water was full of little kids splashing around. And water conducts electricity—

Jason ran down to the fire hydrant to warn the children. But before he could even get off the lawn, I tackled him from behind, losing my head towel in the process.

Jason looked back at me in confusion. "Noah, this isn't a good time for horseplay."

I shook my head. "If we get too close, *we'll* be electrocuted!"

I shouted. "We have to *warn* the kids to leave."

So the two of us stood at the edge of the lawn and screamed at the children: "Hey! You! Yeah, YOU! Get out of the water."

Some of the little kids looked over at us.

"Move it."

Nothing.

"You could get hurt if you don't come up here!"

Right then, the day care's runaway kid made a break across the street, Mrs. Damaschino chasing close on his heels. That meant that getting the rest of the kids away from the hydrant was up to Jason and me. So we waved our arms around. We made threats. We pointed to the broken pole and sparking power lines to show the danger.

And the little children just ignored us. I guess they hadn't studied electricity yet in preschool. All they knew was that there was a cool fireworks show going on right in front of them. It was like that power pole had a hundred sparklers attached to it—and they were all going off at once!

Only two kids paid any attention. One chubby little boy waved back to us. "We're getting WET!" he yelled enthusiastically, splashing the water with his feet. The other kid was a five-year-old girl in a Hello Kitty T-shirt. She stuck her tongue out at us.

At that moment, Jenny bumped into me from behind and pressed something round and cool into my hand. It was the purple-green puck.

"You know what to do!" Jenny yelled.

I didn't move. Or I couldn't move. Either way, I didn't want to use that puck again. I managed to shake my head and say, "I'm sure nine-one-one is on the way."

Instead of arguing, Jenny pointed to the street. By now, Mrs. Damaschino had made it to the hydrant's growing pool and was trying to grab the slippery children. But she was slow and they were quick—and the water was spreading so fast, it was obvious she couldn't get them all before the power line made its deadly connection.

"Noah, someone has to help those little kids now!" Jenny urged. "And that someone is YOU."

Dang it, she's right! My hand shook a little as I pressed the stem on the side of the glittering disc and watched its egg-shaped screen blink into view. And there was the pulsing ball:

ADEPTNESS

I tapped the icon, got the menu, and scrolled to ICE.

Then I stopped. *Is this really happening?*

The fire hydrant gushed, its pool growing ever closer to the power line's spraying sparks. The minivan continued to smoke and *HOOOOOONK*. People screamed. And there, in a tree on Mrs. Damaschino's property, was a small black bird. Was it the black swift? No, it looked more like a black phoebe (*Sayornis nigricans*). Which sort of made sense, because those birds like the water, so maybe it had been attracted—

"Noah!" Jenny shouted. "Do it!"

Oops. And so, for the second time that afternoon, I saw the flashing screen:

ICE

ICE

ICE

9

Downed Power Line Nearly Sparks Neighborhood Tragedy

Firefighter: "Those children will never know how lucky they were."

Santa Rosa—A quiet city neighborhood nearly became the setting for tragedy yesterday. After a broken power pole led to flooding and electrical fires, preschool children flocked to the accident—yet astoundingly, no one was harmed.

At 4:10 P.M., Pacific Gas & Electric technician Sean Kolfax began work on a transformer on Caruthers Avenue. "It was just routine maintenance," Mr. Kolfax told reporters. "But when I went up in the crane and accidentally bumped it against the power pole, all heck broke loose."

For reasons yet to be determined, the pole snapped in half and fell partly onto Mr. Kolfax's PGE truck. The technician was uninjured, but the blow to his truck rendered the crane's controls inoperable, stranding him.

Glen Peabody was driving down Caruthers when the power pole initially broke. Although he was unavailable for comment, Peabody told police that he stopped and backed his vehicle up for safety. In the process, he ran over a fire hydrant and then left the scene on foot.

Children at a nearby residential day care raced to the broken fire hydrant's geyser. Before adults could intervene, the curb quickly filled with children playing in the pool of water.

And that's when things took a turn to the terrifying.

The broken power pole collapsed into the street, its high-voltage wires landing perilously close to the hydrant's water. Residents on the scene rushed to save their children before the expanding wading pool reached the sparking power lines.

"If the pool had expanded that far," said Santa Rosa Fire Chief Ray Loggia, "thousands of volts of electricity could have poured through the water. And the kids who were in it—" The chief paused. "Words can't describe how awful it would have been."

Why *didn't* the gushing water expand to the lethal electric wires? Surprising eyewitness accounts claim that the water froze. "I felt it freeze right over my feet," Damien Huany, 5, told reporters.

Cordelia Shickle, 4, added, "After the water got hard, no one could move. So we all started screaming."

A resident on the scene, Thomas Bright, 41, said he wasn't sure just what he had seen. "IT WAS COMPLETE MAYHEM, WITH SPARKS AND KIDS EVERYWHERE."

Emergency crews arrived on the scene and quickly shut off power to the sparking electrical lines. A ladder was extended up to retrieve Mr. Kolfax, while the children were chipped out of the frozen patch of water by rescue workers.

Asked to explain the incident, Water Bureau Chief Susan Ackerman said, "Lots of factors affect water temperature. It's hard to state with certainty which variables caused the freezing on Caruthers Avenue. My best current theory is that it was an environmental disturbance."

She then added, "I really have no idea."

As for the faulty power pole, PGE spokesperson Sara Arrington was asked how the pole could have become so rotten.

"Horizontal cracks, knots, and decay can all contribute to pole weakening," she said. "Our records show that the utility pole on Caruthers was installed in 1968. That's a long time."

So for now, questions remain and official investigations have commenced.

Looking up from Jason's laptop, I watched the orange-vested city workers replace the broken fire hydrant in the Brights' front yard.

"Okay, so after the power pole fell, there was a crazy chain reaction," I said. "But *why* did the pole fall in the first place? This didn't really explain that."

"Who knows? It was probably woodpeckers." Jason pointed over my shoulder at a blurry photo of the crane and broken power pole. "Hey, I wonder if Coby took *that*." The photo caption read "Electrical Storm, Icy Street—in September!"

"Maybe." Jenny leaned back and looked at me teasingly. "And to think that nobody ever thanked me! After all, *I'm* the one who saved the day. But sadly, the real hero will never be known."

I tried to smile back, but the expression sort of died on my face. The twins just seemed to have the wrong attitude about this whole thing. Don't get me wrong—I was glad the little kids were safe. But even though the purple-green puck was a lifesaver, I still wanted to get rid of it. It was like a double-edged sword. Swing one way, and you cut through a problem. Swing the other way? You cut through yourself!

That puck wasn't mine, it was scary and mysterious, and I didn't want it. Yeah, the adventure we'd had turned out okay, but it was a mistake, a screwup. It was just wrong. My having that puck was in the same category as things like a toilet that won't stop filling, or that moment when you realize your locker combination won't work because you're at the *wrong locker.*

Yet the twins didn't seem to notice (or just didn't care) about any of that.

"Seriously, Noah, *you* could be a hero, but one thing's preventing it," said Jenny.

"What?" smirked Jason. "Courage? Strength? Fashion sense?"

"No, no, and no," said Jenny. "It's that heroes don't slouch."

As I sat up a little, Jason rubbed his hands together. "Topic change! Now, Noah, you may have asked yourself, 'What's *next?*'" He pulled out a clipboard from the chair next to him and handed it to me. "As your manager/best friend, I've written down some ideas for you to think about."

"My manager, huh?" I said doubtfully. Jason's clipboard held a spreadsheet with a list of items and costs. The first one read "Noah's Snow-ah Cones: $3."

This was classic Jason.[4]

---

4. FIELD NOTES: Currency Events

Three years ago, Jason visited my house for the first time. In my bedroom he spotted two wooden swords in my closet. "No way!" he said, picking up one sword and handing me the other. "Where'd you get these?"

"My parents got them at a Renaissance Faire a long time ago."

"Your parents GAVE you swords to play with? My mom would *never* allow that. She'd be afraid that Jenny would cut my head off or something."

Then Jason raised his weapon and cried, "Sword fight!" He swung his wooden blade at my head. (Neither he nor my parents are big on safety.)

I kept reading through Jason's list for the iridescent puck. "Ice-skating: *$20?*" I exclaimed. "Jason, what if someone gets hurt?"

Jason looked at me innocently. "When have I ever gotten you into trouble?"

I didn't bother answering.

Jenny weighed in. "If anything, Jason's not thinking BIG enough. Noah, you just saved a bunch of little kids from being fried. If you want some real money, contact their parents. Ask them stuff like, 'How much is your child's life worth to you?'"

Jason stared at his sister in amazement. "Jenny, you're a genius!"

"True. But I'm also *joking.*" Jenny turned to leave. "How are the two of us even related?"

As you can see, I had a lot of distractions. That is about the only excuse I have for the colossal mistake I was making. I mean, even though a whole day had passed, I *still* hadn't reported my black swift sighting from the day before. Dumb, right? And because of that, another domino fell.

With a clunk, I barely blocked his attack with my wooden blade. But then Jason nearly shish-kebabed me before I could jump backward.

"Fine," I said, buying time. "I'll be the Baron of Santa Rosa, defending my manor. Who are you?"

"Uh," Jason said, raising his blade to eye level. "A kid with a sword?" Then he inspected his weapon more closely. "Noah, these things are still practically brand-new. We could sell 'em to some kids around here!"

And so we did. The point being that Jason doesn't have much of an imagination—unless you need ideas for making money.

10

BEFORE MY FAMILY MOVED THREE YEARS AGO, MY final report card in New Mexico looked like this:

School District: Albuquerque
Student: Noah Grow
Grade: Fourth

KEY
B Beyond Excellent
E Excellent
S Soon-to-Be Excellent

MARKS
B+ Math
B+ Science
B+ Music/Art
B+ PE
B+ Social Studies/Language Arts
B+ Web Technology

Notes: Noah is a delight to have in class. His science fair project, "Endangered Species/Endangered Planet," was the highlight of this year's event.

Yeah, my old school was big on positive reinforcement.

But I practically had to chase my mom and dad down to even look at that report card. That's because we're different from most families. Have you heard of helicopter parents who are always hovering over their children? My mom and dad are the *opposite* of that. They're submarine parents.

Anyway, I finally trapped Mom and Dad at the dinner table. "I think you'll want to see this," I said, sliding the sheet across the table. "It's my report card."

"How'd you do?" Dad asked, pulling his reddish-brown hair back into a short ponytail.

"I got all B's," I said.

"Great!" Mom said.

"But remember, at our school, a B is 'Beyond Excellent,'" I explained. "So a B is actually an A. That means I *really* got all A's."

Mom looked at the sheet. "But these A's are actually *B+*'s."

"So those are actually *A+*'s," I explained.

They had no idea what I was talking about.

Dad proudly patted my shoulder anyway, and Mom smiled. "Great job, Noah. But are *you* happy with it?"

I shrugged. "Sure."

There was an awkward moment of silence.

"Noah," Dad said, "would you please pass the quinoa?"

* * *

New Mexico was where I got interested in birding. I was in first grade, and my science class took part in a school-wide bird-watching contest. The idea was for students to identify as many local species as possible.

Watching birds? How hard can that *be?* That's what my first-grader self thought.

We had a hummingbird feeder at home. I'd been given a checklist with the names and pictures of common local birds, so that afternoon, I sat at the window facing our bird feeder. Mom was out of town, but I'd enlisted Dad to help.

Before long, there was a flash and a whir—a hummingbird darted over and was sucking away at the feeder. (I learned later that hummingbirds don't suck. They actually *lick* really fast.)

"Dad!" I yelled excitedly. "What is it?"

Dad looked at my list. "It looks like a black-chinned hummingbird." He held up the hummingbird's photo. I looked at it, and then back at the bird.

It was a match! With great satisfaction, I marked my checklist.

☑ Black-chinned hummingbird *(Archilochus alexandri)*

That was the first bird I ever identified.

I looked at that little bird, floating in the air. Learning its name made me feel important in a way I never had before. Now *I* knew something about the world that a lot of other people didn't.

I was hooked.

So I started reading about birds. I learned some amazing stuff. For instance, many birds barely sleep. Others, like the Alpine swift, might stay up in the air for two hundred days at a time. That means they sleep while flying.

Lots of Asian parrots hang upside down when they sleep, like bats. And as for hummingbirds, they conk out so hard at night that they look dead.

I started stalking our neighborhood, my eyes peeled for finches, sparrows, and hawks. With one of Mom's old digital cameras, I took shot after shot of bird after bird. Then I compared my photos to the checklist.

More check marks.

Finally, the last day of the contest arrived. With Dad's help, I printed out my best bird photos and labeled them, starting with the black-chinned hummingbird.

In two weeks, I'd checked off twenty-seven birds on the list.

And I won! My prize was a certificate and a pair of cheap binoculars. I carried those binoculars *everywhere*. I started watching birds even more carefully. Some birds were flashy-looking. Others seemed boring at first, but then behaved in startling ways. And other birds were just weird.

I got new checklists and new bird books. I built birdhouses. I joined the local Audubon Society.

So yeah, I had birds on my brain.

Mom and Dad liked how birding got me outside. And since

my parents designed playgrounds for a living, every summer took us to a new spot where they had jobs. That gave me the chance to see lots more birds in different habitats.

I saw whistling ducks and sandhill cranes. I saw a tough little black-masked loggerhead shrike—also called the "butcherbird." And once at a playground in Florida, I spotted a flying squadron of brown pelicans. Suddenly one of the pelicans dropped from the air as if it'd been shot. It hit a nearby lagoon like a rocket and disappeared. But a moment later, there was the pelican again—with a giant fish hanging from its beak.

Pretty awesome.

At first, knowing a lot about birds made me sort of cool at school. I mean, think about it: ALL little kids love fuzzy, furry, feathery animals. So in first grade, I was instantly "somebody" for winning the bird-watching contest.

But it didn't last. The more I got into birds, the more things at school changed. Boys got more interested in sports and girls. Girls got more interested in—

Actually, I have no idea what girls are interested in.

But *nobody* stayed totally interested in fuzzy, feathery animals. Nobody but me. I didn't mind. Really. Because as my friends migrated away, I had even more time for birding.

You can probably see where this is going. Over time, even *my* parents noticed how I almost never had other kids over. And they must have got worried. So the day after we moved to Santa Rosa, Mom and Dad drove me to a public swimming pool.

This was annoying, because I wanted to scope out some new Northern Californian species.

"Sorry, Noah," Dad said. "But you probably won't see anyone your own age at a bird refuge."

"And honey," Mom encouraged, "the Aquatic Center will be a great place for you to meet other kids before school starts."

Yay, I thought, looking out the car window. Yet amazingly, my parents were right. (Don't you hate that?) I'd just started swimming around the pool when a boy in bright-red swim trunks ran down the high-dive board. He leaped from the end, flew through the air, and cannonballed into the water right next to me.

I floundered to the shallow end, coughing, while a teenage lifeguard yelled at the jumper. Afterward, the cannonballing kid swam over to me.

"Sorry about that," he said, brushing water from his face. "I never even saw you!" He glanced poolside. "Man, I'm so lucky my mom didn't catch that. But how about you? Is one of your parents going to yell at me?"

"Nope," I said. "My parents just dropped me off."

"Cool," the boy said. "I'm Jason, by the way." He swam backward into the deeper water. "So, your parents trust you here all alone, huh? They must not be very strict."

"Well," I said, "they never ask to see my report card."

Jason was stunned. "Dude, you're *so* lucky." He flagged down a black-haired girl who was walking past. "Hey, Jenny, listen—this guy's parents never ask to see his report card!"

Jenny looked at me with her pale blue eyes. As she did, I realized she looked a *lot* like Jason—but somehow, that wasn't a bad thing.

"Yeah, right," said Jenny skeptically. "So what does your mom say when grades come in?"

I imitated my mom, using her mellow meditation voice: "*Great job, son. But the important thing is that* you're *happy with it.*"

Jenny laughed and sat down at the edge of the pool, kicking her legs in the water. "What about your dad?"

Encouraged, I deepened my voice. "*Son, we're proud. Keep up the good work. But only if* you *want to.*"

"Can you believe it? Your parents sound like the best," said Jason. "What's your name, anyway?"

So that's how I met the twins. From the start, they were fascinated with my mom and dad. My parents were *different*—and Jenny and Jason thought of my family as an exotic species.

And the twins *loved* that my parents are professional playground designers. They even have their own company—Free Range Playgrounds. At our new home in Santa Rosa, the backyard quickly sprouted models of play structures that my parents dreamed up. Jenny and Jason never got sick of coming over to play on—or gawk at—these creations.

One of the twins' favorites is a model that looks like a jungle gym for creatures from another world. It's the first version of my parents' most popular invention—the Möbius Fun Climb.

To picture the Möbius Fun Climb, think of a big, wide metal slide that's been hammered flat and turned on its side. Now cover its flat surface with footholds and handholds for climbing.

Got it? Finally, imagine that long climbing strip is going in a circle. And as the strip goes around, it slowly twists over 180 degrees. That means that as you climb, you start vertical, work to a flat surface, and then go back down again.

If that sounds like it would be hard to play on, take it from me: IT IS. Back in New Mexico, when I was seven, my parents talked me into climbing on one of the first Möbius Fun Climbs.

My parents have a funky way of looking at the kids (like me) who play on their equipment. It's like they're judges at a dog show, rating the different entries.

"It's okay, honey, you can do it," encouraged Mom, taking a photo. (At this point I was hanging sideways and whimpering.) "We trust you to make good climbing decisions."

So I tried to reach the next handhold, but it was like trying to climb an optical illusion.

THUMP.

I fell off the Fun Climb and onto the bark dust. Mom rushed to me, while Dad typed on his laptop.

"I'm proud of you for taking that risk," Mom said. She was brushing bark dust off me, the sleeves of her peasant blouse tickling my nose.

Dad glanced up. "Remember, Noah, it's by making mistakes that you learn. Are you ready to try again?"

Using me as their guinea pig (or guinea *monkey*), my parents changed the Fun Climb to something the average kid probably wouldn't break his neck on.

Probably.

Like I said before, my parents are just not big on safety. Their Web site's banner says, *"When we banish dragons, we banish heroes. THIS is where kids find risks and overcome their fears!"*

Under that is a photo of me clinging for dear life to the Möbius Fun Climb. (From the expression on my face, you can tell that I "found risk.")

But it's not *all* bad. I mean, my parents let me go bird-watching almost anytime I want. They're not paranoid and freaked-out that kidnappers are lurking everywhere. And so I actually have way more freedom than other kids my age.

But that *doesn't* mean that I get my own cell phone.

"We don't need to keep tabs on you," Mom said. "And neither should anyone else. You're better off without society's tethers."

"Tethers?" I asked. "Like the poles with big yellow balls at the playground?"

Mom smiled. "Yes. And like a big yellow ball, you're better off with no strings attached."

"Your childhood is a gift," added Dad, "and we want you to enjoy your own amazing adventures."

"But I don't really WANT to have amazing adventures!" I argued. Plus, no cell phone meant I was missing out on some good bird-watching apps.

And of course, now that I had the mysterious purple-green device, there was no way I was telling my parents about it. But not because I thought they'd take it away. No, it was because they'd just think that puck was the most "amazing adventure" ever.

And how annoying would *that* be?

11

Jason scanned the school hallway. "Is Mrs. Sanchez ready for you *yet*?" he whispered.

The bell for the end of school had rung ten minutes ago, but handfuls of kids were still hanging around, waiting for rides home or club meetings to begin.

I took another impatient peek through the window in the science classroom's door. Inside, a woman in a white lab coat was *still* talking to an eighth-grade girl with a nose ring.

"It looks like we have to wait a little longer to talk to her," I said. "Hey, Jason, did you know that nose rings are okay to wear at school?"

"Sure," said Jason. "That's why I'm getting one next week.

Anyway, if you finally get in, I'm staying out here. That lady scares me."

"That doesn't make any sense," I said. "Mrs. Sanchez is, like, the most inspiring teacher at this school."

"Yeah," Jason agreed. "She inspires *fear.*"

Two laughing sixth-grade girls stopped at a nearby locker, so Jason and I moved away to avoid them. It's weird being in a school's hallways after hours. What was noisy and crowded a little while ago was now quiet and deserted.

And yet there were still clutches of kids lurking in odd pockets and classrooms. Over here was the Chess Club, its members huddled silently over their boards, plotting their opponents' destruction. Over there was the Debate Team, with kids shouting things like "Resolved!" and "Oh, no, you DIDN'T!"

But as we walked around, Jason and I couldn't find an empty, unlocked classroom. So finally we gave up and went to the bathroom. (That means we *walked* to the bathroom, okay?)

I pushed through its swinging door, and the two of us stepped into a short tiled hallway. I held up my hand for a moment to listen, but the bathroom was silent.

As the door slowly swung shut, Jason started talking. "Are you going to tell Mrs. Sanchez about it?"

"No!" I whispered. "We have to keep that a *secret—*"

A familiar voice interrupted me: "You have to keep WHAT a secret, Noah?"[5]

Footsteps came toward us, and I turned around and looked up. (After all, Coby Cage is pretty tall.)

"No secrets here," I murmured.

"What's that?" Coby said, holding a hand to his ear. "Squeak up!"

Jason made a sudden move to the door—but before he could make a run for it, Coby grabbed him and spun him into the bathroom. He went flying and slammed against a tiled wall, then crumpled to the floor.

It was horrible. Jason was lying on the *bathroom floor*!

"Oops, sorry," said Coby. "I didn't mean to throw you that hard." He *sounded* sincere, but I'm sure it was sarcasm. Then Coby brushed past me (warning "Don't go anywhere!") and went out the bathroom door.

---

5. FIELD NOTES: I Become a Rule-Breaker

Our school allows nose rings but bans innocent stuff, like skateboards and soft drinks. So if I'd asked for permission to bring a mysterious puck with dangerous properties to school, the answer would've been "No."

Actually, the answer probably would've been "Huh?"

But I had important questions about the puck, like "WHAT IS THIS THING?" So I needed to talk to a logical adult—and at our school, that was Mrs. Sanchez.

So, in the name of science, I'd brought the puck with me. Jason didn't know it was in my pocket. He thought I was just going to ask Mrs. Sanchez some *hypothetical* questions.

(And my decision would lead to more not-so-hypothetical dominoes falling.)

I ran to Jason. His eyes looked slightly crossed. "Jason? Can you hear me? Are you okay?"

"Noah," Jason croaked. "Avenge me."

"What's that?"

"I might be dying." Jason's eyes slowly uncrossed. "And you know that means *you* have to punish the person who did this to me."

"But we're not even related," I protested. "Why can't Jenny do it?"

Jason thought about that for a moment. "She's tough, but unreliable. No, you have to be the one to do it."

I glanced at the bathroom door. *Where did Coby go?* "How about if I just tell Mrs. Sanchez?"

Shaking his head sadly, Jason groaned. "You really don't understand how to avenge someone's death at all. Forget it—I'll just go ahead and live."

Then the bathroom door swung open. Coby was back!

"Good news," he announced. "This place is totally deserted." Coby gave Jason a penetrating look. "Hey, both of you were at that car accident two days ago. So I'm guessing the 'big secret' is that you know something good about it." Then he paused and held up a finger. "Just one sec."

Coby went to the first toilet stall and pushed open its door. (It's always good to double-check for witnesses before killing other students.)

The stall was empty.

Jason twitched like he was going to make a run for it again. "Don't even think about it," Coby warned, going on to the second stall.

Please let there be someone there, please let there be someone there, I prayed.

That one was empty, too. But someone *had* stuck a wet piece of gum on the stall door, and now it was attached to Coby's hand. Cursing, he pushed up the sleeves of his long-sleeved T-shirt and went to a bathroom sink.

"Okay, you two goofballs—start talking!" Coby demanded, as the water turned on automatically.

The other goofball stayed quiet, so I did too.

"Fine, have it your way." Coby sounded almost happy to be given the chance to beat the truth out of us. Whistling cheerfully, he squirted soap on his hands and lathered up. (For a troublemaker, Coby sure had great hygiene.)

Rubbing my scar anxiously, I realized something important. Jason and I didn't *have* to take a beating. Remember?

Gently, I eased the purple-green puck from my pants pocket. Holding it at my hip, I pushed its stem. As the screen opened, I tapped the round icon and the menu tumbled down, its gray words disappearing and appearing—

And then, there it was: ICE.

I held my thumb over the word just as Coby spotted what I was doing. "What is that? A phone? Are you gonna call your mommy? I'm afraid she can't come right now. Mommy's busy at the *playground*."

"Wow, that was cold," Jason said.

I clenched my jaw. You know the rule: *Never talk about someone's mother—especially when that someone has a squished purple-green puck with mysterious properties.*

So I tapped the screen and it started to flash:

ICE

ICE

ICE

12

WHY DID I LIFT THE PUCK TO MY HEAD? I DON'T KNOW. Maybe I finally understood that hiding or running away from my problems wasn't working. Or maybe I saw that it was time for me to stand up for who I was and what I believed in.

But mostly it was because Coby said I was calling my "mommy."

So as the puck cooled off in my hand, I held it to my ear like a phone without thinking.

This was not the smartest thing to do.

The puck's frosty feeling hovered for an instant in my hand—then, like rainwater finding a gutter, it flowed right down my ear canal. Instantly, a mini-blizzard was swirling inside my head.

"Blouw!" I blurted. (I was trying for *"Whoa!"* but my tongue was already frozen.)

Inside me, an arctic blast was roaring through my body—and I needed to get rid of it! Pointing my right fist, I looked at the water pouring from the sink and imagined funneling the cold at it.

Meanwhile, Coby was almost done rinsing soap from his hands.

"*Blouw!*"

A blast of pale-blue power swept out from my fist and surrounded the sink. There was a brittle, tinkling sound, and Coby turned pale. That's because his big wet hands were stuck in the faucet's icy waterfall. And as more water came out, more ice formed around them.

"Hey!" Coby said, tugging at his hands. "You FROZE me? Not fair!"

"No, it's not fair," agreed Jason. "It's *awesome.*"

I enjoyed the moment—I was in *control*! But I was also overflowing with freezing energy. As the bitter cold filled my body, my trembling thumb hit the puck's stem to close the screen and (hopefully!) cut off its power supply.

But where could I send all of the ice already in my system? It had to go *somewhere*—

I swung my right fist at the first toilet stall and shot a short blast.

Shwink-CRACK!

Then I brought my left fist up and did the same thing to the next door.

Shwink-CRACK!

The icy blue bolts flew right through the metal stall doors, seeking out the water behind them. The toilet bowls must have frozen solid instantly.

It felt great. Even though I sensed that most of the energy was gone now, I kept firing. "Yeah!" I yelled, blowing another door open. "Take that!" But before I got to the last stall, there was an outraged squeak.

The door flew open, and a small, round boy bolted from it. How'd Coby miss him? He must have lifted his feet up when he heard us—and now was sprinting out of the bathroom in a blur. The kid almost looked familiar, but he vanished before I could place him.

"Whoa!" said Jason. "He moves fast for a little guy."

As for me, I exhaled cool mist into the air and looked at the puck. *This thing is really amazing!* I thought, turning to Coby.

"Wow, sorry about all that before," he said, grimacing. It took me a second to see that Coby was trying to make a friendly smile. It looked more like he had a face cramp.

I gripped the puck a little tighter and smiled back. My anger was giving way to a new feeling. There Coby was: frozen and helpless. And now it was MY turn to make threats. Maybe I'd tell Coby I was going to turn him into a full-body ice cube. Then I'd make him apologize for being such a jerk. And most of all, I wanted to make him sorry for ever messing with me!

I tightened my fists, looking forward to what would happen next—

"Noah?" Jason was looking at me like I was a total stranger. "Are you okay? You have a really weird expression on your face."

Whoa. I'm like, gloating, or something. But that's not like me. I'm totally not a gloater. And just like that, my wish for revenge went away. My hands unclenched and I took another, warmer breath. "I'm good. Thanks."

Coby had silently watched all this while frozen in place. And then, sensing it was safe, he asked, "Hey, did that sparkly thing help you do all that?"

Argh! Why did I have to get a smart *nemesis?*

From my expression, Coby must have guessed the truth. "Does it do other things too? Like, can it make you fly?"

I raised my hand in annoyance. "Jason asked the same thing—"

But Coby must've thought I was going to shoot more ice his way. Desperately, he wrenched his hands, and with a brittle *crack,* he broke free from the frozen sink. Coby staggered backward, his hands still stuck together in icy handcuffs.

And then big, tough Coby Cage ran out of the bathroom faster than the little kid a moment before.

Wow. My thirst for revenge was overshadowed by a new, better, bigger feeling. "Victory!" I cried. "Jason, can you believe it? We beat him! High five!"

Jason left me hanging. "Oh, right," I said, dropping my hand down. "You *were* touching the bathroom floor. Gross."

He shook his head and gave me a look that said *Do I have to explain everything?*

So I thought about it . . . and a second later, realized the horrible truth: *Now Coby knows about the puck.*

13

Ten minutes after I'd frozen the school's toilets, I peeked inside the science classroom again. The girl with the nose ring was gone, and Mrs. Sanchez was grading papers at her desk.

I pushed the door open and cleared my throat. "Excuse me, Mrs. Sanchez, do you have a minute?"

Mrs. Sanchez looked up. "What can I do for you, Noah?" she asked briskly.

MRS. VICTORIA SANCHEZ *(Elegantis eruditius)*

APPEARANCE: Average height. Average build. Above-average presence.

VOICE: Calm and quiet, yet somehow always commands attention.

PLUMAGE: Long white lab coat. Straight black hair. Cool gray eyes.

RANGE: Mrs. Sanchez is only ever seen on school grounds. Like many teachers, she may not exist away from her classroom.

SOCIAL BEHAVIOR: Unknown.

STATUS: High. All younger life-forms know not to misbehave with her.

I stepped through the door and walked closer. "Uh, I was wondering if you'd take a look at something for me?" And with that, I set the still-cool puck on her desk.

Another teacher might have laughed or rolled her eyes or said, "What IS that?" But Mrs. Sanchez picked up the puck and began examining it. Her fingers immediately found its handhold, and a moment later, she pushed the stem on the side.

As the puck's screen blinked into view, it gave off its familiar greenish glow.

"Do you have *specific* questions about this object, Noah?" Mrs. Sanchez asked, frowning at the puck.

"Well, for one thing, I was wondering about its screen," I said. "Some people have trouble reading it."

"But not other people?" Mrs. Sanchez gave me a keen glance, then got up and placed the puck on a scale. Weighing it produced frowning. Next, out came a magnifying glass. Mrs. Sanchez then pored carefully over every inch of the puck. She looked at its back last, and said something like, "It's a quincunx."

"Sorry?"

Mrs. Sanchez glanced up and motioned me closer. "Look—there's a pattern of five indentations on the back of this object. See how they're arranged?"

Leaning in, I peered at the puck's magnified surface. I saw four slight dips, forming the corners of a square. A fifth indentation was in the square's center. It was the same pattern used for the number 5 in dice or cards . . . or dominoes.

Mrs. Sanchez rose and walked to the whiteboard. "There's a word for that pattern." She grabbed a marker and wrote it out: *q-u-i-n-c-u-n-x.*

I looked at the word, and I liked the look of it. After all, the purple-green puck wasn't really a puck. It was something more mysterious. More interesting.

Something like a *quincunx*!

Moving to a microscope, Mrs. Sanchez positioned the lens over the back of the quincunx and looked in the eyepiece. Once in a while, she'd adjust the focus, but was otherwise motionless.

I stood in front of a lab table covered with beakers, and twiddled my thumbs.

She kept staring. And staring.

Restless, I experimented with twiddling my fingers. Then,

since Mrs. Sanchez wasn't looking, I stuck my arms out to the sides. Starting with one hand, I tried practicing a dance move Jason taught me called the pop-and-lock.

You know the one—you start by flipping your finger and wrist joints on one hand, then let the "ripple" move across your body? Of course, I didn't want to use the pop-and-lock at one of our school dances. (I'd never even been to one!) Instead, I thought it might be a solid addition to my arsenal of Fake-Fu moves.

But as I made my first pop, my hand hit a beaker on the table behind me. The beaker spun to the edge of the table and almost fell, but I lunged wildly and just caught it. As I did, my elbow hit *another* beaker, which smacked into a third one. Suddenly, I was whirling around a table of clattering beakers, trying to prevent massive destruction. By the time I was done flipping out, Mrs. Sanchez was coolly looking at me.

"Sorry, Mrs. Sanchez," I said. "None broke."

"That's fine," she said. "But, Noah, I need to ask you a question."

Uh-oh.

"S-sure," I stammered.

She pointed to the quincunx. "Is this object yours? And if it's *not* yours, where did you get it?"

Double uh-oh.

In a nervous rush, I said, "I don't know where it came from or who it belongs to." Mrs. Sanchez kept looking at me with no change in her expression. It was like I hadn't said anything at all.

"But I found the quincunx under a bush," I added helpfully.

Her eyes narrowed. "You discovered this object beneath a shrub?"

"At the bottom of a hill," I added, blushing because it sounded so stupid. *Looks like Jason was smart to stay out of here,* I thought miserably. "I don't know what it's for exactly. But maybe it's like a phone?"

Mrs. Sanchez waved me over to the microscope. "If so, then I can tell you one thing for certain." She gave me a look. "If you're right, then this quincunx is a cell phone."

I stopped. Was she joking? Mrs. Sanchez *never* joked!

"What I mean," she continued, "is that this would be a truly *cellular* phone." She stepped away from the microscope and motioned me to her seat.

I sat down and looked through the microscope's eyepiece. For a moment, I was blinded by the quincunx's glittering reflection. As my eyes adjusted, I saw the glitter was coming from dozens of clear shapes.

These were tiny pentagons, tightly packed against each other like a puzzle. Faint double lines formed a border around each pentagon. Inside these lines was a single, round form, a tiny ball of purple and green. And this is where the quincunx's glittering came from—those balls were like miniature colored suns.

I recognized what I was seeing. *We had just been studying this in class.* With a gasp, I pulled my head back from the eyepiece.

"It should look familiar," said Mrs. Sanchez. "After all, those are actual cells."

I bent down over the eyepiece again. "So the outsides of the cells are membranes?"

Mrs. Sanchez didn't say anything. She wanted me to figure it out.

And if these are cells, then the bright balls in the middle—

"And the round, glittery things are . . . nucleuses?"

"*Nuclei,*" corrected Mrs. Sanchez. "Keep looking."

So I did. I stared and stared, and at first, I didn't understand what I was looking for. But after about thirty seconds, I saw it.

The cells are moving.

The movement was very slow, but there was no mistaking it. As my eye swept over the purple-green cells, I saw one of them doing something familiar: it was splitting into two parts.

"I think I just saw one of the cells reproduce!"

"That wouldn't surprise me at all," Mrs. Sanchez said. "Because this device is alive."

14

It's not that I freaked out. But after Mrs. Sanchez told me that the "device" was alive, I muttered something about my parents picking me up. Then I grabbed the quincunx and ran out of the science class.

So, okay, maybe I freaked out a *little*.

When Jason saw me burst into the hallway, he chased after me. The two of us sprinted and didn't stop until we were off-campus. Finally, I bent over panting and Jason—who wasn't even breathing hard—phoned his dad for a ride. (Ever since Jenny's accident, Mr. Bright drives the twins almost everywhere.)

"Okay," said Jason, hanging up. "Why are we running?"

Still huffing, I managed to ask, "Do you . . . want to know something . . . really *weird*?"

Jason looked thoughtful. "How should I answer that?"

Gingerly, I pulled the quincunx out. "This thing is alive."

Jason wasn't impressed. "So its battery isn't dead?" he scoffed. "Big deal!"

"No, no. It's not not dead. It's ALIVE."

Jason just looked at me. "Huh?"

* * *

Pock! Pock! Pock!

The air hockey board hummed in the garage as the black puck bounced back and forth. Jenny and I were playing a game, but it was mostly just to cover the sound of our voices.

"So you didn't tell Mrs. Sanchez about ICE?" Jenny asked, shifting her paddle to her left hand. Then she caromed the plastic puck off two of the rink's edges, and it spun past my paddle, into the goal.

Pock! Pock! PING!

Another point for Jenny.

"Just practice," I protested, fishing the puck out of the return slot. "And no, I didn't say anything about that to Mrs. Sanchez. We're the only ones who know what it can do."

"And Coby Cage," corrected Jason, looking up from his cell phone. "Hey, Jenny, what about Dad?"

Pock! Pock! Pock!

Jenny's eyes never left the puck. "I think he was too distracted during the power pole accident to notice anything. But you can add Mrs. Sanchez to your list, because now she knows *part* of the story."

Pock! Pock! Pock!

Jason shook his head impatiently. "This is such a waste. Noah should just announce what he discovered and then sell that—that—what do you call it now?"

"A quincunx."

"How could I have forgotten? Anyway, that quincunx could make us *rich*."

"I've got a better idea," said Jenny, her eyes lighting up. "Noah should let a charity or a scientific organization have it. Think of all the good it could do!" She lunged forward.

Pock! PING!

This time, the hockey puck shot through my goal so fast, it ricocheted out and went flying through the air. "I'm done. You really don't know what 'practice' means, do you, Jenny?" I asked.

Handing Jason my paddle, I turned and faced the garage shelves. They were piled with board games: Monopoly, Battleship, Risk, chess, dominoes—

Dominoes.

I thought about how I'd found the quincunx, and what I'd done with it. I thought about the unintended effects my actions had.

And that's when I came up with my Domino Theory. You know—how we're surrounded by invisible dominoes? And they can knock over other dominoes that we don't even know about?

I threw my shoulders back and made a decision. "We're *not* selling the quincunx," I announced. "And we're not giving it to charity or science either."

The twins stopped playing and looked at me in surprise.

"I'm the one who found this thing," I said. "So stop telling me what to do. And *I* want to keep it a secret. Let's see what we can figure out on our own. Okay?"

Jenny sucked her lips in and bugged her eyes out. "O-kay," she agreed reluctantly, positioning her paddle in the middle of the board.

"Fine," said Jason. "I'll go along too." Giving his sister a cocky look, he added, "And now, let me show you how to play this game."

Pock! PING!

Jenny yawned and left the air hockey table. "You two are really terrible at this."

* * *

"Okay, Noah, time to get organized."

Jason sat at his desk, with his laptop and the quincunx in front of him. Although I knew the quincunx was alive, I didn't worry that it would sprout legs and run off. It may sound dumb, but I almost had a feeling the quincunx was happy to be there. Even so, I couldn't take my eyes off it. Was it breathing? What kind of temperatures did the quincunx like? Did I need to water it or something?

Meanwhile, Jason made a simple chart on his screen.

What We Know	What We Don't Know
The quincunx was lost.	WHO lost it?
It lets Noah shoot ice.	Does it do anything else?
The quincunx is alive.	What? HOW?
Only Noah can use this thing.	☹ Total rip-off!
Coby and Mrs. Sanchez know about it.	So now what?

We stared at the questions for a moment. Then we looked at the quincunx.

"We can't answer *any* of these," Jenny said.

"We're just gathering information," said Jason. "Noah, let's start with you. When you dial ICE, how do you feel? Besides being cold, I mean."

I thought back. First, I froze the backyard pool. Then a pitcher of water and the overflowing fire hydrant. And then earlier today in the bathroom—

"The cold feeling is stronger if I'm near water," I said. "So ICE gets boosted by anything that can be turned into, uh, *ice*."

We talked about how long the different connections had lasted, and how I'd held the quincunx each time. Jason typed in this information while Jenny tapped her chin thoughtfully. "Okay, we're getting somewhere. I'll bet the next time you use this thing, it'll be less crazy. Now, what about the other words you see in its menu? Do you think the same things apply to them?"

I shrugged. Lifting the quincunx, I tapped the oval screen and scrolled. As before, ICE was there, but it was no longer in dark letters. Now it joined the other menu choices, which were all written in a hazy light gray and sliding in and out of the list.

"Okay, these are alphabetical. There's ABSQUATULATE, CEILOMETER, DIVARICATE—"

"Go to 'F' and see if there's one that makes you fly!" said Jason.

I sighed, and kept scrolling. As I did, my finger slipped into the center dip on the back of the quincunx. And a new screen appeared:

NEW ADEPTNESS CHOICES?

"Hey, check it out! The quincunx is asking me a question!"

The twins huddled around me, which was silly, since they couldn't see anything. So I read the question aloud.

"How stupid is this thing?" asked Jason. "Of *course* you want a new adeptness. But how can you text back?"

Jenny shot him a warning look. "Careful, Jason. The quincunx might have voice recognition software. Say something to it, Noah!"

I cleared my throat awkwardly. "Hello?"

The pop-up screen remained.

"Try answering the question," suggested Jason.

"Right." It felt strange, but I spoke to the quincunx. "Um, yes?"

The pop-up window popped out of sight. But newly revealed were two menu choices that I *could* select:

FIRE [SAPID]
FIRE [TEPEFY]

"Uh-oh," I said.

"What?" Jason was practically hopping up and down with excitement. "What's it say now?"

"There's two choices, but both say FIRE—"

"Fire power!" Jason exulted. "Dude, it's every kid's dream. We *have* to go find out what it does!"

I gave Jenny a *please talk some sense into your brother* look.

"Well, we DID just come up with some safety guidelines," she said.

I grimaced and pretended to choke on something. But I was also thinking about what I'd learned about the quincunx so far. If I kept the connection short and made sure that the quincunx was far away from my ear . . .

"C'mon, Noah," Jason begged. "You know what your girl-friend, Mrs. Sanchez, would say: *experiment.*"

"First of all, Mrs. Sanchez is NOT my girlfriend," I said. *And second of all, if I did have a girlfriend, her name would be Anemona.*

I looked at the twinkling quincunx. I'd used it three times so far and nothing bad—okay, nothing *very* bad—had happened yet. Maybe Jenny was right.

I made a decision. "Inside or outside?"

"Outside," said the twins simultaneously.

"Let's head over to Berkeley Park," said Jenny. "There's a big pond there, in case we need it." As Jason ran out the door, Jenny gave me a look.

"What?" I asked.

"Nothing," she shrugged. "You just surprise me, that's all. Now stop scratching your scar, and let's go."

* * *

Even from the pond, I could hear the kids on the other side of the park. A shout carried from the playground: "I'm next on the Möbius Fun Climb!"

That kid's got a death wish, I thought. Then I looked down at the sparkling quincunx in my hand. *And maybe that makes two of us.*

Loud chirping from a nearby tree caught my attention. Peering up into its branches, I spotted the blackish-purple sheen of a male great-tailed grackle (*Quiscalus mexicanus*). And just like that, I broke out in a cold sweat. *THE BLACK SWIFT.* Now it had been two whole days since I'd spotted the bird. Discovering the quincunx was making me forget to take care of the most important thing of all!

"Are you okay?" I could barely hear Jason's shout. He was standing behind an elm tree about fifty yards away.

"You look kind of freaked-out, Noah." Jenny was on a nearby paved trail. She was leaning her chin on her palms, watching me. "Getting cold feet?"

"More like a heat rash." I took a deep breath. "Preparing to access FIRE!" *And RIGHT after this, I'm reporting my black swift sighting.*

Jenny nodded, and Jason slid behind his tree.

In case you're worried, yes, I knew it was dangerous to play with FIRE. So our foolproof plan was for me to throw any little sparks or massive fireballs that might come my way into the pond. Getting ready, I accessed the menu and thought about my two choices. I didn't know what "tepefy" meant, but figured "sapid" was just a misprint for "rapid." You know, like "rapid fire"?

So I made my decision, and the quincunx screen flashed.

FIRE [SAPID]

FIRE [SAPID]

FIRE [SAPID]

Did the quincunx just vibrate? Almost as soon as the quincunx screen started flashing, I pressed its stem to disconnect it. But for an instant, I had the feeling that the quincunx was linking me to . . . something.

So I stood there at the water's edge, waiting for something to happen. And while I waited, I could hear laughter, leaves rustling in the wind, a barking dog.

The great-tailed grackle chirped.

But nothing happened with the quincunx. There was no rapid fire or slow fire. There was nothing at all.

"Well, THAT was a letdown," said Jason, sticking his head in my refrigerator. (He *loves* scrounging for food at my house.) He pulled out a plastic container. "Whoa, this tofu needs medical attention! Anyway, I thought you were going to throw a fireball for sure."

"I don't get it either," I said. "And I don't know what you think you're going to find in there—my parents only buy pro-biotic food."

Jason reached into a cupboard and started pulling out jars. "I don't even know what 'probiotic' means, but it sounds deli-cious—"

And then a warm jolt shot through my entire body and my mouth started watering. "Whoa!"

"Noah?" said Jenny, spinning to face me. "Are you okay?"

"*My moubt is pull of pit,*" I said.

"It's FIRE!" yelled Jason, ducking behind the refrigerator. "Go outside, quick!"

But it was already too late. My eyes had locked on the jar that Jason was holding. It held my focus—and I could feel energy slowly gathering inside of me.

I gulped. "*Dumdinth goin' to 'appen!*" I warned, drooling a little as my mouth flooded with saliva.

My eyes widened—now the warmth inside me was rush-ing to my face, to my mouth. It was almost like I was going to cough and barf at the same time. Then I closed my eyes and sneezed loudly.

It was probably the loudest sneeze I've ever sneezed.

As I opened my eyes, Jason and Jenny were looking back and forth between the jar in Jason's hand and me.

Gingerly, I swallowed. My mouth felt normal again.

"Dude, *something* just shot out of your mouth," Jason said, looking at the jar. "And it hit this peanut butter."

Jenny rolled over and carefully took the jar from her brother. Unscrewing the lid, she looked inside, then turned the jar so we could see.

Inside, it was still full of peanut butter. It looked normal enough, but . . .

Jason broke the silence. "If we're going to experiment, let's *experiment*." He grabbed a knife and smeared some of the chunky peanut butter on a thick slice of multigrain bread.

He held it up to his nose and sniffed. "Smells okay!"

"Jason," warned Jenny. "Be careful with that peanut butter!"

But he bravely bit into it anyway. As Jason started to chew, a look of horror slowly came over his face.

"Don't joke around," warned Jenny. "Are you okay?"

Jason's eyes bulged. He flung the bread into the sink and yelled one word: "Fire!" I grabbed the fire extinguisher from next to the stove and aimed it at him. "What is it? What's wrong?"

Jason turned on the water tap and shoved his mouth under it, ignoring our pleas. He drank and drank and drank some more. He finally stopped slurping, just to breathe.

"Jason, where's the fire?"

"In . . . my *mouth*," he gasped. "It's really . . . spicy . . . peanut butter!"

When Jason finally pulled away from the water, his face was red, but he seemed okay. "Well, now we know one thing." He took a deep breath. "Whoever made the quincunx has a bad sense of taste."

"Or a good sense of humor," I added. "Jenny, can you look up 'sapid'?"

Jenny pulled her phone out and pecked at it. "It says here that 'sapid' means 'strong flavor.' Oops." She smiled at her brother, who was now fanning his tongue with air. "I guess that *was* an important detail, huh? But Noah, you said there were *two* FIRES. What was the other one?"

I told her, and Jenny reported back: "Tepefy: to make tepid or lukewarm," she read. "Huh? Why would we want to do that?" Her phone beeped, and as Jenny read the incoming text, her face grew serious. "It's Coby—but how'd he get my number?"

Jason paused his fanning. "How would I know? That guy can hack into anything."

"It doesn't matter *how* Coby did it," I said impatiently. "What does he SAY?"

Jenny just turned her phone around.

I read Coby's text. Then I read it again. (But it said the same thing the second time.)

TELL NOAH 2 BRING FONE 2 SKOOL TMRW—
OR I TELL EVRY1

I was sweating and my heart hammered in my chest. *What do I do now?*

"This is not good," said Jason. "He just wants to take the quincunx and be an outlaw who shoots ice and . . . and makes spicy peanut butter."

"Maybe." Jenny frowned in disgust. "Coby breaks so many laws, it's not even funny."

"Huh? What laws?" I asked.

"The laws of *spelling*," Jenny said. Her thumbs flew over the phone's screen. "I'm writing back."

Good luck in the Spelling Bee.

15

I WOKE UP STILL FEELING GUILTY. YES, THE LAST FEW days had been crazier than the rest of my life added together. But the quincunx had fogged over what I was *supposed* to be doing.

As the morning sun shone through my window, it reminded me of what was truly important. Its rays hit a black-headed Canada goose that was gazing out from my "Birds of North America" poster. Eighty years ago, these geese were hunted so much, they were almost extinct in the United States.

But then people—just regular people—decided to help. They set aside land and food for the birds. And the goose population rebounded, big-time. Today, there are millions of them.

"Noah, *you* can make a difference," the goose on the poster seemed to be saying. "Do it!" Or maybe that was just me talking to myself. Either way, it was a good pep talk. I rolled over and grabbed the completed form on my nightstand.

RARE WILDLIFE SIGHTING FORM

Date of sighting: September 7

Rare wildlife name: Black swift (Cypseloides niger)

Number of animals seen: One adult bird

IMPORTANT: Photos/video/audio are strongly encouraged to verify accurate claims.

Was a photo taken? No.

Was video recorded? No.

Was audio recorded? No.

How was your species ID made? I saw the bird and heard its call.

Describe the physical features that you think identify this animal: I saw a black swift, about twenty centimeters long, with a fan-shaped tail. Also, I heard a *plik-plik-plik-plik* call.

General site of sighting: Noyd Woods Nature Preserve, Santa Rosa, CA

Land owner of site: The Noyd family

Specific location/description of habitat: A small river runs through Noyd Woods. At the base of Pleasant Ridge, it has a waterfall—Noyd Falls. The black swift seems to be nesting behind that waterfall.

IMPORTANT: Are there any plans to build near this site? No.

Has this species ever been seen at this location? I don't think so.

What wildlife background and experience do you have that can give validity to your claim? In first grade, I was named my school's "Birder of the Year." I have memorized the scientific names of almost all North American bird species. Oh, and my science project last year, "The Drake Equation," was about local wood ducks.

If needed, will you accompany a fish and wildlife official to this location? Yes!

Even though I knew what I'd seen, filling out my contact information on the back of the form still made me nervous. What if the person who read it just dismissed me as some kid who didn't have any evidence to prove his claim?

Last night, I'd given the same information online at the Department of Fish and Wildlife Service Web site, but to be safe, I'd printed out a copy to mail the old-fashioned way, too. So after double-checking to make sure the details were right, I sealed the form in an envelope. Then I hopped out of bed, threw on a T-shirt and cargo shorts, and checked the clock. I only had a minute, but I wanted to read a little more about my new friends at the nature preserve.

From my shelf, I picked up a book about black swifts that I'd bookmarked.

> "—I thought there could be a black swift nest in a local sea cave. But I found I could only get to the spot at low tide. After timing my approach to the cave between waves (and still nearly drowning), I was rewarded by the sight of a moss-bordered nest high on a rock ledge. And there, looking calmly down at me like a little feathered prince, was a baby black swift."

Wow! I closed the book and sighed. And then an unwelcome thought intruded—Coby wanted me to bring the quincunx back to school.

Fine, I thought defiantly. *I'll do that.* I went to my closet and reached down into my dirty clothes hamper. My fingers felt through my laundry, then closed around a small cardboard box. Yep, my clothes hamper was the perfect hiding place. After all, I did my own laundry. So who was ever going to dig around in my grimy T-shirts and sweat socks? Nobody!

Of course, since the quincunx was alive, I couldn't just throw it in next to the laundry. That would be, like, animal cruelty. (Or was it a plant?) Either way, I'd punched a few holes into a cardboard box that a compass had come in, then set the quincunx into it.

"Sorry about that," I murmured, opening the box and slipping the quincunx into my pocket. I was feeling good and confident. Sure, Coby obviously wanted to get his hands on the quincunx. Who wouldn't? But I was pretty sure that the quincunx would protect me.

Of course, the device was sort of unpredictable—so maybe I was stepping into a trap that I wasn't seeing. If so, there was one sure way to avoid that trap: I could just skip school.

And of course, my parents would just *love* that. No, seriously, they would. Mom and Dad think that it's "healthy" to break the rules sometimes. For a moment, I closed my eyes and imagined myself hopping on a big black motorcycle in front of our house.

"No helmet?" Dad says, as the motorcycle's engine rumbles. "Way to go, son!"

Mom looks hopeful. "Are you going to play hooky today, Noah?"

"I don't *play* hooky, Mom," I say, revving the engine. "I take it very seriously."

Dad nods happily. "That's my boy—born to be wild. Now go have yourself an *ADVENT*—"

I opened my eyes. I *HAD* to go to school. True, Coby might somehow get his hands on the quincunx and then use it for some terrible crime. But we had a math test today that counted for 15 percent of our final grade. So I really didn't have any choice in the matter.

Grabbing my letter, I went out and ate a bowl of locally grown oatmeal with my parents. Then I hoisted my backpack and headed out. I walked down the block to the blue public mailbox and dropped my black swift report in its slot.

Next, I headed for my bus stop. It was time to face Coby Cage for the third time in three days. And since I'd also just done something that would hopefully protect an endangered species, I was feeling *pretty* good about myself.

I straightened my glasses. My step was firm. My chin was up. I was ready for my appointment with destiny. But to anyone watching, I probably just looked like a big-eared kid with glasses walking to the bus stop.

The bus lurched to a stop. The door swung open, I hopped aboard, and there was Mr. Berry. At least I *think* he was there behind his sunglasses, hat, and the thick black beard covering most of his face.

Scanning the seats, I saw the usual younger kids up front.

The farther to the rear I looked, the older the kids got. Near the very back, Anemona Hartliss *sigh* was nodding in agreement at something someone was telling her.

And Coby's usual seat in the back was (thankfully!) empty.

I looked at Ronnie, who had his head stuck in a math book. (He's the only kid I know who stresses about homework more than I do.) "S-sorry, Noah," Ronnie peeped. "Big test today."

One thing to know about Santa Rosa is that the kids here ALWAYS sit in the same seats. It's a really big deal. And if someone *changes* seats, everyone notices. It's like changing nationalities. So Monique Wilson and her little brother always sat behind Ronnie and me. But both of them were absent, so as the bus jerked onward, I walked past my usual spot and slid into their empty seat.

I remembered Jason's question from the day I found the quincunx: *"Why does Coby hate you so much, anyway?"* I wished I had an answer. I mean, Coby was meaner than a substitute PE teacher. He was smarter than a chess club captain. But scariest of all, Coby was more unpredictable than a cheap firecracker. You just never knew when he was going to pop up—

"Hi, Noah," said a soft voice behind me.

I smelled lilacs.

Turning, I saw a girl with a bundle of red hair tied at the back, her glossy lips curved in a smile. Anemona Hartliss. The One. I opened my mouth, but no words came out. My mind was an empty closet. I touched my scar. Seconds passed like hours . . . and then I got a brilliant idea:

"Hi," I answered.

Anemona laughed like I'd said something clever. It sounded like someone gently shaking a pot of gold at the end of the rainbow. Then she leaned forward and rested her elbows on the back of my seat. This brought our faces closer together.

From such a short distance, I was stuck with a problem: *Where do I look?* Her amazing lips? No. Her big eyes? No! Finally, I settled on her nose. After all, how much could a nose distract me?

"I have a question for you," Anemona said. "Can you keep a secret?"

I managed to nod, concentrating on her nose.

Anemona smiled. "Here's my secret. You know how some people think I'm an airhead just because I'm popular?"

"What?" I protested. "No!"

Anemona clucked her tongue. "That's sweet, but you know it's true. What no one knows is that I'm actually a total secret nerd. I mean, I love reading books and stuff, like science fiction. And I love that British TV show, *Dr. Whom.*"

I grinned, then quickly closed my mouth since my teeth are so big. "It's okay, I'm a secret nerd too," I said. "Only the secret got out."

Anemona smiled at me—and it was like being hit with a dazzling beam of light. "You're *funny*! Why didn't I know that you were so funny?" She poked me in the arm with her finger, touching my scar. "So what about you—do you have any *other* secrets?"

I could only gulp. *SHE JUST TOUCHED ME.* And in that moment, my theory that "nobody likes the person who likes them" just seemed stupid. Of course they did—the evidence was right here!

Anemona laughed again. This time it sounded like silver coins trickling into a forest brook. "Oh, come on, you can tell me anything." She leaned closer, her eyes twinkling. "How about this: Is there anyone at our school who you *like*?"

She gave me a slow wink, and my heart almost stopped. Actually, I'm pretty sure it *did* stop.

Then Anemona quietly added, "Listen, I'm really sorry to bring it up, but I hear you found something at Noyd Woods?"

Wait—what?

I cleared my throat. "Did Jason tell you about this?"

"Mmm-hmm," Anemona agreed. She cocked her head like a cardinal (*Cardinalis cardinalis*) inspecting a berry. "And he said you probably wouldn't mind if I looked at it for a second."

I absently patted the quincunx in my pocket. This was all very unexpected. When did this happen? Did Jason call Anemona last night? I took a deep breath to calm down, and her lilac smell grew stronger. (Or maybe it was honeysuckle. Whatever.)

"If you let me take a little peek at it, I'll be your best friend," Anemona said teasingly. "Your best friend in the *whole* world."

Lame, right? Well, guess what: *I believed her!* All I had to do was show Anemona the quincunx, and one thing would lead to another. Next thing you know, we'd start hanging out all the time. It'd be like in those romantic comedies, the part where the big power ballad blasts.

In my mind, the music would play while Anemona and I sat on the bus together, laughing about *Dr. Whom.* Then we'd text each other all day and hold hands as we rode the bus home. And heck, Mr. Berry worked for the city! He could marry the two of us at my bus stop, and then all the kids would throw flowers out of the school bus windows. . . .

Whoa. This was getting away from me. But still, Anemona was right there, with her big green eyes and a friendly smile. She was flirting—with *me*!

"Just one little peek?" Anemona asked, raising her eyebrows encouragingly.

I glanced around. Nobody was paying any attention besides maybe Ronnie Ramirez. (Although he was facing forward, Ronnie was shaking his head slowly.) I pulled the glittering quincunx out and cradled it in my hand like a baby bird that'd fallen from its nest. "This is it," I whispered.

Anemona squinted. "Can I see it?" I moved the quincunx a little closer to her. "I mean, can I *see* it?" She held out her hand,

and as she did, I noticed that Anemona's green eyes had little flecks of gold in them.

I gingerly handed her the quincunx. She took it and leaned back in her seat. I turned more and put my arm over the seat. Then Anemona pulled a little notepad and a purple gel pen from her purse. She turned the quincunx over carefully and looked at its back with a little frown.

And then she started taking notes!

How observant, I thought, impressed. *She'd make a good birder.*

"Thanks," Anemona said a minute later, putting away the notebook and pen with a *click-click.* Then—without even looking at where it might go—Anemona tossed the quincunx backward, over her shoulder.

"Hey!" I yelled in horror and surprise. My purple-green quincunx was sailing through the air, turning end over end in slow motion.

It'll be broken, crushed . . . KILLED.

The quincunx flew back, back, back—

—and then, magically, a hand reached up from behind a seat and plucked it from the air.

I slumped in relief. *Yes! Saved!*

The hand holding the quincunx stayed in place while its owner sat up where I could see him. Guess who? Yup, that's right: Coby Cage.

16

"WHAT?" JENNY SPUTTERED FURIOUSLY. HER EYES lit up like road flares. "How could you have *lost* the quincunx already, Noah? HOW?"

The twins had been waiting for me at school. And as soon as I got off the bus, they knew something was wrong.

"Listen, Jenny, I didn't *lose* it," I said. "I know exactly where the quincunx is." And right then, Anemona walked past us. She paused like she wanted to say something to me, but Jenny gave her such a murderous glare, Anemona just kept going.

"Noah," Jason said, "please tell me that Anemona didn't have anything to do with this."

"I was tricked!" I said guiltily. "Anemona said *you* said it was okay for her to see the quincunx."

Jason acted like I'd accused him of murder. "Dude, why would *I* tell someone *our* secret? How could you believe that?" I just looked at him. "Okay, that was a pretty good move on her part," Jason admitted.

But Jenny wasn't letting me off that easily. "Noah, why do you act like a little schoolboy around her?"

"Technically, I *am* a schoolboy," I said, but neither of them was listening anymore. Because Coby Cage was walking by— with the quincunx glittering in his hand.

Coby glanced over at us. "Hey, kids," he said cheerfully. Then he squinted up into the sun and got a nasty gleam in his eye. "Nice day we're having, huh? It'd be a real shame if it *cooled off.*"

Coby paused dramatically. "You know what I'm talkin' about? I wonder if it'll *cool off.*"

We knew what he was talking about.

Coby walked off, chuckling.

"You may as well tell us how he got it," Jason said quietly.

So I tried to explain.

* * *

After Coby caught the flying quincunx, he'd handed something small to the two girls in front of him, Mindy and Beth. (You might remember Mindy as the girl who's "secretly" in love with Jason.)

MINDY and BETH *(Histrionicus vociferus)*

APPEARANCE: Always together.

VOICE: All vocalizations delivered as high-pitched questions? Like this?

PLUMAGE: Bright, trendsetting.

RANGE/SOCIAL BEHAVIOR: Flanking or flocking. (That means Mindy and Beth are always either flanking Anemona or flocking to a larger group.)

STATUS: High.

Mindy took the item from Coby and unfolded it—a twenty-dollar bill. She placed it in her pink handbag, and gave Anemona a nod.

I couldn't believe my eyes. "You stole for *money*?!" I demanded.

"I didn't steal anything," Anemona said innocently. "Trust me, Coby's not going to KEEP it. He'll just look at it, and then you'll get it back." She tossed her hair dismissively. "Besides, it's not yours—you *found* it. What's so special about that thing anyway?"

I was so upset, I didn't even wonder how Anemona knew that I'd found the quincunx. Instead, I slumped in my seat. "You wouldn't understand."

Anemona gave a little snort. "You might be surprised." Then she got up—even though the bus was moving—and walked like a queen back to her usual seat in the rear of the bus.

And Mr. Berry didn't even yell at her!

Meanwhile, I could see Coby bent over in his seat. The quincunx's green glow lit his face from below, making him look like a monster. *Yikes.* I turned back around and found myself facing Ronnie Ramirez. He held up his wristwatch. "Th-that only took her f-five minutes."

So much for my appointment with destiny.

* * *

As I finished telling my story, Jenny clenched her fists. "So Anemona made goo-goo eyes, and you HANDED the quincunx to her?"

"Yeah." I shrugged sarcastically. "The goo-goo eyes get me every time." As Jenny got ready to strangle me, Jason planted himself between us.

"What's done is dumb," he said. "The question is, *What do we do now?*"

I tried to look at the positive side. "Look, we're probably safe. After all, Coby won't be able to use the quincunx."

"But what if he *can?*" asked Jenny. The three of us looked at one another. Coby Cage was bad enough on his own. But Coby with ice? He'd freeze the principal just as a warm-up.

And then he'd come after us!

The twins must have been thinking the same thing.

"We've got to get that quincunx back," said Jenny.

Jason nodded. "It could be dangerous." He turned to me. "Just in case Jenny and I don't make it, will you tell our dad our final words?"

"You're always so dramatic," I said. "Fine, what do you want? Something like 'I love you'?"

"No, no," Jenny said. "What good would that do? Tell him our last words were, 'Coby Cage killed us.'"

By now, the last buses had pulled away. Except for a couple of kids walking across the parking lot, everyone had headed to homeroom. "When should we try to get it back?" Jason asked.

I thought. "My guess is that we've got till the end of school. Coby'll probably want to keep this secret to start with."

The homeroom bell rang. The three of us turned to go inside—and there stood Coby, waiting for us. So much for *that* theory.

Jason and I jumped back in surprise, but Jenny moved toward him with a gleam in her eye. "So, you want to return what you stole?" she said, holding out her hand.

Coby laughed in disbelief. Then he pointed at me. "Why do you twins even hang out with this *third wheel*?" He glanced meaningfully at Jenny's wheelchair. "Get it?"

I looked around in vain for an adult, but there's never a teacher around when you need one. Coby thumbed the quincunx's screen. "You probably should have dressed warmer today, Noah," he said. "Now let's see . . . G, H, and aha, there it is—the letter I. For 'Ice.'"

"Wait." I was shocked. "How can you *read* that?!" The quincunx had betrayed me. Of all the people to reveal its secrets to, why my archenemy?

"Amazing, huh?" Coby brought the quincunx a little closer to his face. "You're not the only smart one. I can read and write and everything. But whoever programmed this thing sure can't spell."

"*Psst*," hissed Jason. "Should I make the call?" He showed me the screen of his iPhone. He had already pressed 9-1, and his finger was hovering over the "1" button.

"There's no time," I whispered back. "We should run for it."

"*I* say we jump him," Jenny said. "It's three to one!" Amazing, right? Jenny was on fire—she had more guts than Jason and me put together. Anyway, while we argued about what to do, Coby brought the quincunx up to his ear. ICE was on the way.

I took a step backward, even as Jenny continued forward. *Dang it, so much for my escape.* I may be a coward, but I wasn't leaving the twins to fight Coby alone.

But there was just one little problem—I don't actually know how to fight.

"Spread out!" Jenny yelled.

Jason stopped in his tracks. "Why?"

Jenny rolled her eyes in exasperation. "So he can't freeze us all at the same—"

"Too late!" I cried. Coby had a strange smile on his lips, and he was already pointing his hand at me. As Coby closed his fingers into a fist, pale-green circles of energy began rippling around it.

I felt cheated. *What a rip-off! The quincunx didn't give ME any green energy circles when I used it.*

Coby was staring at the green circles around his fist and laughing diabolically. Something bad was about to happen. Something REALLY bad.

"Jason!" I yelled. "Hit the 1! Hit the 1!"

17

AND THAT WAS WHEN I SAW THE MOST HORRIBLE Thing I've Ever Seen in My Whole Life. (And I'm including the time Ronnie Ramirez blew milk out his nose.*)

The circular green waves covering Coby's huge fist began spreading. As more circles appeared, they started working their way up his arm. "Awesome!" Coby crowed. Then he pointed his shimmering green fist at me. "You're toast, Noah. *Frozen* toast."

So I had three choices:

- ☐ Tell Coby that "*frozen toast*" was impossible. (You can either *freeze* bread or *toast* it, not both.)
- ☐ Attack Coby with my Fake-Fu.
- ☐ Run away as fast as possible.

---

*Let's just say that Ronnie had a cold.

Did you know there really *is* a fast-running bird called the roadrunner? The real roadrunner (*Geococcyx californianus*) looks more like a woodpecker than a cartoon ostrich.

Anyway, when the cartoon roadrunner "*beep-beeps*" and then races off, his feet are just a whirl of speed. And that was *me*, as I sprinted across that parking lot at a breakneck pace.

But as I ran, a voice behind me kept getting louder and louder.

"*. . . oah! Noah! Noah!*"

Someone was catching up to me—but at my speed, that was impossible.

"*NOAH!*"

Now I could even hear heavy breathing as my pursuer got closer—so I put my head down and poured it on. I pretended I was outrunning an avalanche, a lion, an enraged volleyball coach. I was practically flying!

And then a hand tapped me on the shoulder. *Coby!* How had he done it? Did he freeze the asphalt and skate after me on its slick ice surface? I was about to become frozen toast. But I wasn't going down without a fight. So I stopped running, spun around, and dropped into a battle crouch. (True, I don't know what a battle crouch is, but I was ready for anything, especially if it involved crouching.)

But it wasn't Coby who'd tapped my shoulder. It was *Jason.*

"Dude." Jason looked awfully pale. "You have to come back."

"W-wait a minute," I gasped, my heart racing like a hummingbird. "H-how did you even catch me?"

Jason looked puzzled. "You're really slow. Look, you barely made it out of the parking lot."

I looked around. I'd run about sixty yards. So much for being a roadrunner.

"Hurry," urged Jason. "Or just come as fast as you can." He turned and effortlessly ran back across the school parking lot—and back to Coby Cage.

I followed. And what I saw next was horrible. It was awful. It was unspeakable. Let me tell you about it.

As I ran back, I spotted the iridescent quincunx on the sidewalk. Its oval screen was still flashing—Coby must have flung it away at some point. I began to detour to pick it up, but Jason grabbed my arm and pulled me away.

"Look!" he said, pointing.

Someone had barfed a big pile of what looked like blackberry waffles on the sidewalk.

No, that's not the unspeakable part. This is:

The quincunx's green energy waves had replaced Coby's entire body! You know those Visible Man anatomy figures? The ones with clear plastic skin, so that you can see all the bright-red muscles and freaky organs and tissues and tendons and bones on the inside?

Now imagine a life-size version of that. And even though the life-size version has clothes on, you can see through those, too! Finally, imagine that the figure isn't made out of plastic. It's made of an *actual* person.

Suddenly the Visible Man made a sound: *"What is happening?"*

"Aah!" I yelled and jumped. "What *is* that?"

Jenny turned to me. Her eyes looked glassy, like she might faint. "THAT is Coby."

"HELP ME!"

"Aah!" This time, Jason and I both yelled and jumped as the Visible Coby took a step toward us.

I tore my eyes away from the pile of Coby parts. Then a movement caught my eye—a mane of flaming-red hair. *Anemona.* She was just beyond Jenny, lurking behind a plum tree. Anemona's eyes locked with mine—and then, they slid down to something bright and shiny on the sidewalk near her.

The quincunx.

"Jenny!" I cried in a panic. "Look!"

Jenny spun, spotted Anemona, and gave her wheels a powerful spin. As she did, Anemona took two steps and bent toward the quincunx.

As Anemona reached down, Jenny blocked my view. Then she got to Anemona, there was a brief tussle, and the quincunx fell to the sidewalk again. As it did, Jenny spun 180 degrees around. Like lightning, she reached down with her hand and batted the quincunx to me like a—

Well, like a hockey puck, actually.

The quincunx skittered across the pavement—past the Visible Coby (*yuck*)—and came to rest against my shoe.

"Nice shot!" I yelled, crouching to pick the sparkling disc up. (I knew all that crouching would pay off.) The screen was still flashing, so I quickly pressed its stem to end the connection. *But will that reverse Coby's visibility problem?*

"Hey, Anemona," I said triumphantly, waving it over my head. "Who's got the quincunx *now*?"

Anemona just looked at me, expressionless. There was an uncomfortable silence.

"Well, it's *me*," I concluded.

"Calm down, Noah," said Anemona, frowning. "*I'm* the one who said that you'd get your toy back." She tossed something on the sidewalk. It was a twenty-dollar bill. "And I didn't do this for the money."

She glanced at Visible Coby, who was now just sitting on the sidewalk and holding his skull in his horrible see-through-ey hands.

"Oh, gross," Anemona said matter-of-factly. Then she wrinkled her nose in disgust and walked off.

I called after her halfheartedly. "And I don't like you anymore, either." I clenched the quincunx a little tighter. So it didn't betray me after all. And in its own bizarre style, the quincunx had found its way back to me.

As Jason ran and grabbed the twenty, Jenny flicked a finger

at Anemona like a switchblade. "Not only did she break Noah's heart," she said to Jason, "but this is all *her* fault. And I'm going to get her back for it."

I was touched that, even in all that craziness, Jenny was so protective of me.

"Easy, sister," said Jason, happily tucking the money into his pocket. "Sometimes you get a little too hung up on getting revenge."

"We'll just *see* about that!" Jenny snapped.

"Oh, man." That was me, looking at Coby. Remember when you imagined the Visible Man? Now try picturing him becoming un-visible. It happened really fast—first, his bones disappeared, then his slimy organs. (Was that gray thing a spleen? Or his liver?) And then I just had to look away. I'm telling you, it was unspeakable!

A moment later, Jason said, "It's safe now, Noah." I looked back around, to see Coby seated on the sidewalk in front of us. He looked exactly the same as before, except now he didn't appear cocky at all. Not even a little.

I pointed to the puddle of barf on the sidewalk. "Who had the blackberry waffles?"

Jason raised his hand and hiccupped.

As for Coby, he lifted his head up from his hands. "I don't feel very good," he groaned. Then he looked up at me. "And you're going to be sorry when I tell my brothers about this."

"Why?" protested Jason. "What did *Noah* do?"

Then, to my amazement, Jenny leaned down and touched Coby's arm. "We should get you to the nurse's office."

I guess she sees through his "tough guy" act, I thought. But Coby didn't move. Neither did I. Because I was still wondering about something: *How'd Coby read my quincunx?*

Oh, and one more thing—remember when I passed the quincunx on the sidewalk, just before Anemona tried to steal it a second time? I forgot to tell you what was flashing on its screen. It was the Adeptness command that Coby had chosen.

He hadn't picked ICE at all. The screen read:

ICK

ICK

ICK

18

THE BELL RANG. HOMEROOM HAD OFFICIALLY STARTED.

What a lousy morning, I thought. *My first tardy!*

Jason looked toward the school. "I guess we should just go to class now?"

Nobody had a better idea, so we left Coby, sitting on the pavement by himself next to Jason's blackberry barf. He looked so miserable, I almost felt sorry for him.

Almost.

The only things stopping me were two little details. You know, robbery and attempted murder.

* * *

By third period, it was time for Science, and that meant Mrs. Sanchez. And it was going to be awkward. After all, I'd basically sprinted out of her classroom the day before.

As usual, Mrs. Sanchez was standing outside her classroom

door, greeting students. As I passed by trying to act normal, she just gave me a little nod.

Inside the classroom, the lights were off. A green map of North America was projected from a laptop onto a screen at the front of the classroom. As the bell rang, Mrs. Sanchez closed the door and we all quieted down. "Today we're going to begin a lab experiment about causes and effects," she said. "But first, please take a look at this map. The green shows how much wild habitat there was in North America back in 1775. As you can see, there was a *lot* of it."

With a remote control, Mrs. Sanchez clicked through to other maps from 1800, 1825, 1850, and 1875. With each new slide, the green shrank more and more.

Next, a big picture of a bird appeared on the screen. It looked like a mix between a dove and a robin.

"*Ectopistes migratorius!*" I whispered in surprise.

Mrs. Sanchez continued. "This is a passenger pigeon. In 1775, there were billions of these birds in North America."

A new slide now, of a huge flock of the pigeons flying over a prairie. There were so many birds, they blotted out the clouds, the sun—practically the whole sky.

"That's Photoshopped!" said Mindy Grimsley.

"It looks unbelievable, doesn't it?" Mrs. Sanchez shook her head.

Now another photo, this one showing men with shotguns posing by what looked like huge mounds of clothing. It took a moment for us to realize these were piles of dead passenger pigeons.

"I'll spare you the details," continued Mrs. Sanchez, "but the story of the passenger pigeon is not a happy one. Because the birds always stuck together, they were easy targets for hunters. By 1896, there was only *one* last remaining flock of wild passenger pigeons. Word spread, and people traveled from near and far to take that last opportunity to hunt the birds.

"And in a single day, nearly every bird in that flock was shot."

"Whoa," said Nick Stomp. "How many were there?"

"About a quarter-million," said Mrs. Sanchez. "Four years later, the very last wild passenger pigeon was shot in Ohio by a teenager. He hoped this would get his name in the newspaper. It did."

"But how is that even l-l-legal?" asked Ronnie.

"It's hard to understand today," Mrs. Sanchez said, "but it wasn't against the law to kill the last wild passenger pigeon. In fact, there was glory in it. The idea of protecting an endangered species wasn't common." She glanced at me. "Back then, even bird-watchers shot birds to study them."

A few students eyed me suspiciously.

"So, to sum up—although passenger pigeons were once plentiful, a brief period of overhunting caused a permanent effect."

Then she clicked to another map, this one with just a fraction of green color. "This is how much wildlife habitat we have in North America today."

Up in the front row, Shannon Hayes raised her hand. "Wait, most of the forests are gone now. So would the passenger pigeon have gone extinct even if it *hadn't* been hunted?"

Mrs. Sanchez turned on the classroom lights. "Now *that's* a very interesting question. And it makes for a perfect lead-in to the experiment we're going to start today. . . ."

A strong feeling came over me. No, not love for Mrs. Sanchez (no matter what Jenny says!). It was *determination*. There was no way I was going to let my black swift end up like the passenger pigeon.

At lunch, Jenny, Jason, and I leaned our heads together over a cafetorium table. I'd just told them about the ICK I'd seen at the scene of the slime.

Jenny tapped the table with her fork. "Maybe ICK is a useful choice."

"Yeah," agreed Jason. "Like if you needed to gross out your enemies or something!"

"Or maybe Coby knew that *i-c-k* isn't how you spell ice," said Jenny, "but he chose it anyway because he thought the programmers entered it wrong."

I rolled my eyes. "Yeah, but neither of you can read the quincunx's screen. So why could Coby?"

Jason had an idea. "The quincunx is alive, right? So maybe it was actually protecting you. See, the quincunx knew Coby was a threat—so it sort of disabled him."

Just then, I noticed Coby in the lunch line. He was queasily looking at the slices of pizza under the heat lamps. "Looks like he's feeling better," I said, pointing with my chin.

And then I felt a jolt of shame as I remembered how I'd run off, leaving the twins to face Coby alone. *I'm such a chicken.* Before I could apologize for my flight instinct, Ronnie Ramirez popped up next to Jason, holding a food tray.

"I just h-heard something that you guys sh-should know," he said, glancing nervously at Jenny.

"Ronnie, how do you *always* know what's going on?" asked Jason. "You must have your fingers in, like, fifteen pies at a time."

Ronnie looked down at his hands. "Th-that's impossible," he objected. "Anyway, someone was t-talking about something cool that Noah has."

"And who *was* it?" demanded Jenny, making Ronnie practically flinch. (Her outspoken personality flusters him.)

"Um . . ." he said.

"Was it Coby?" I asked.

"H-h-h—," gulped Ronnie.

"*Maybe* it was Coby?" prompted Jason.

"It-it-it—" Ronnie was starting to sweat.

Jenny couldn't stand it anymore. "It was *Coby*, wasn't it?!"

Ronnie nearly jumped out of his skin "Y-yes! Yes! It was Coby!"

"Really?" I asked. One minute Coby's a wreck, the next minute he's planning a comeback.

"N-no, wait. Not really," said Ronnie. "It was *uh-uh-Anemona*." His shoulders slumped in relief.

Anemona? I looked across the cafetorium—and I spotted her in line for the cashier, right behind Mindy and Beth. As I watched, Anemona stepped around them and walked right past the cashier as if she'd already paid.

But she *hadn't.*

As Anemona casually approached her usual table, her cold green eyes met mine. Then, very slowly, she winked.

* * *

After lunch was Social Studies with Mr. Feely. I barely had time to sit down before an office aide came in and handed the teacher a call slip.

"Noah?" Mr. Feely said, handing me the note. It read:

Please send Noah over at your earliest convenience.

M. Sanchez

I took the note and then sat back down at my desk. Mr. Feely gave me a surprised look. "Noah," he said, "I think she means *now.*"

"Oh!" I blushed and looked at the note again. "Why didn't she say so?" I grabbed my backpack and hustled out.

Moments later, Mrs. Sanchez looked up from her desk. "Hello, Noah. Please close the door. Now, we need to talk some more about your quincunx. Did you happen to bring it with you to school today?"

I paused. *She must've found out what happened to Coby.*

"Yes." (What can I say? I'm an honest person.)

Mrs. Sanchez nodded like she'd already known. "Noah, I've had time to think about the quincunx—and it's important. VERY important. For starters, we know that it's made from a substance that's *alive.* Do you know what that means? It represents a turning point for science. The technology used to make it is . . . it's mind-boggling."

She glanced at the whiteboard, and something she'd written there caught my eye: "The Drake Equation."

Well, THAT'S weird! Why was a teacher quoting my own science project back to me a whole year later? I mean, sure it'd been good, but was it *that* good?

But then I looked at what Mrs. Sanchez had written underneath "The Drake Equation"—and I couldn't see what wood ducks had to do with this:

$$N = R_* \times f_p \times n_e \times f_l \times f_i \times f_c \times L$$

Mrs. Sanchez moved to the board. "Noah, have you heard of the Drake Equation?" she asked.

"Well, yeah," I said. "I thought I invented it!"

She gave me a dry look that said *This isn't the time for humor.* "I see. Regardless, *this* equation is named for the astronomer Frank Drake. His work led to this formula for estimating how many other intelligent species might be in our galaxy.

"The *N* represents the number of civilizations that we might be able to communicate with. The other symbols represent a number of determining factors, like the number of stars and planets. And using the Drake Equation, *N* can equal about ten thousand. In other words, Drake concluded that there could be as many as ten thousand alien civilizations in the Milky Way *alone*."

"So no ducks are involved?" I asked, wanting to be sure.

"Not unless they're intelligent ducks from another star," she said. "Noah, let's talk about your quincunx. Of course, it's a man-made device, not one from outer space. But the Drake Equation is useful for getting us to think about all of life's *possibilities*.

"Your device shows an incredible new form of technology— the kind of thing we used to think could only exist in a science-fiction story. But where did the quincunx come from?"

I held up my hand. (Hey, I was in science class, after all.) "Jenny Bright thinks it's a prototype for some new handheld device," I said. "And Jason thinks . . . well, never mind what Jason thinks."

"Yes, but what is *your* theory, Noah?"

Of course, I'd thought about this quite a bit. But I wasn't going to tell my science teacher that one possibility was that the quincunx was magic. "I really don't know where the quincunx came from," I admitted. "But I am pretty sure that my having it is an accident."

Mrs. Sanchez gazed out the window with a faraway look in her eyes. "Our challenge is to answer these questions and discover the device's true nature. Noah, working together, we can experiment on your quincunx using the kinds of scientific inquiry we talk about in class. Together, we'll learn as much as we can. *Together* is the best way to make sensible decisions for everyone."

That was quite a speech, I thought. *Did she practice it?*

"Plus, you can even earn extra-credit points for helping us. Not that you need extra credit."

Okay, something was wrong—*very* wrong. Mrs. Sanchez *never* gave extra credit!

"Uh, who is 'us'?" I asked.

Mrs. Sanchez blinked. "Pardon me?"

"Well, you said 'we can experiment' and 'you can help us.' Is that you and me?"

She nodded absently. "Yes, just you and me, and perhaps a few of my scientist colleagues."

I got a sinking sensation. "Mrs. Sanchez, have you told anyone else about the quincunx?"

She reached her hands out to me. "Noah," she said, "the secrets your device contains can be used for the greater good. It's too important for us to keep to ourselves. For example, maybe the quincunx can even help prevent the next bird species from going extinct. Do you see?"

I said I saw. (But really? I didn't.)

Mrs. Sanchez reached her hands out even farther. "And now, may *I* have the quincunx, please?"

I stepped back. Almost by reflex, my hand touched my scar. "I . . . I'd rather not."

Mrs. Sanchez's face hardened. "Noah," she said. "The school handbook clearly spells out the district policy on students and electronic devices. When a teacher requests a student's device, the student is obligated to turn it over."

Then Mrs. Sanchez gave me a gaze that could have melted steel. "I'm officially requesting that you give me that cellular device."

She held her hand out for the final time.

19

Yes, I gave Mrs. Sanchez the quincunx. (What else was I going to do? Run out of the classroom again?)

"Thank you, Noah," she said, taking the quincunx and setting it on her desk. "You did the right thing. Now we can show this to an expert."

"You know an expert on quincunxes?"

"No," Mrs. Sanchez said. "But this device came from *somewhere,* so there must be someone who knows about it."

"Well, I've been using the quincunx for three days," I pointed out. "So right now, that sort of makes *me* an expert."

Mrs. Sanchez's eyes lit up. "Good point." She moved her laptop in front of her. "Noah, how exactly did you *use* it?"

I was confused. *Did she just trick me, Anemona-style?*

But I trusted Mrs. Sanchez . . . more than Anemona, anyway. This was, after all, a scientific mystery that needed solving. So I started talking. At first, I just meant to tell her about freezing the swimming pool. But from there, I went to the broken fire hydrant, and the next thing you know, I sang like a canary.

In other words, I told Mrs. Sanchez everything. As I talked, she typed rapidly on her computer. And when I finally finished talking, I felt a *lot* better.

Mrs. Sanchez looked up at me from her laptop. *It's actually a relief to tell all this to an adult,* I thought. *But what will she make of all this?*

* * *

The inside of the school psychologist's office was painted a cheery light blue. There, behind his desk, Mr. Gillespie peered at me.

MR. CHIP GILLESPIE *(Psychologae gnoma)*

APPEARANCE: Very short. Glossy, helmetlike hair; thick, bushy beard.

VOICE: Nonthreatening. Poses sentences like a question?

PLUMAGE: Red-framed glasses. Often wears cargo shorts with a dress shirt.

RANGE: School-wide.

SOCIAL BEHAVIOR: Typically spotted trying to empower students.

STATUS: High-ish, due to his popular therapy dog companion—a black Lab named Spencer.

Mr. Gillespie's office windows looked out on our school's front lawn. There, gulls cawed and dive-bombed a garbage can, hoping to find food.

The psychologist watched me watching the birds. "Those seagulls make quite a racket, don't they, Noah?"

"There's actually many kinds of gulls," I said. "Those ones are Californian gulls, but they have a wide geographic range." (I almost added *They're even the official state bird of Utah*, but I didn't want to seem like a show-off.)

A flurry of gull calls rang out—*kyow kyow kyow!*

"That almost sounds like laughter, doesn't it?" asked Mr. Gillespie. I nodded cautiously. "If you had to guess, would you say those gulls are laughing at anything in particular?"

That would be me, I thought grimly. But I didn't say anything. Talking too much was why I'd been sent here in the first place.

Mr. Gillespie leaned forward and patted Spencer, who was lying on a cushion near his chair. Spencer, the school's therapy dog, roams the hallways getting petted by everyone and listening to baby talk (*lots* of baby talk). But somehow, Spencer keeps his dignity—even with the bright-pink Hello Kitty bandanna tied around his neck.

Mr. Gillespie studied his computer screen. "Mrs. Sanchez says that you've been having quite the adventure. Has anything like this ever happened to you before?"

Oh, great. He thinks I'm losing it.

"No," I said firmly. "I never had *any* adventures until a couple of days ago."

A few moments passed. Mr. Gillespie looked at me with an expectant expression, stroking his beard.

"And that's when you found your magic device?" he finally said.

"It's *not* magic!" I said, frustrated. Then I realized something: *maybe the quincunx really IS magic.* "It's just—there's nothing I can say about it that will make sense."

Mr. Gillespie nodded. "Look, you're a smart young man, so let me be honest with you. The way I see it, these are the possibilities."

He began ticking points off on his fingers. "*One*, you're lying to me. *Two*, you're lying to yourself. *Three*, you've received a head injury that makes you think the device you found has supernatural powers. Or *four*, you're suffering from a neurological condition that makes you believe this."

I held up my thumb. "There's a fifth explanation."

"Hmm?" said the psychologist. "Oh, that you're telling the *truth*? Yes, I suppose there is that, too." Mr. Gillespie pushed himself away from his computer and wheeled his chair closer to me. "Noah, you say you've used this device a few times now. How did that make you feel?"

I was tired. *What could it hurt to tell him?* "The first time I used the quincunx, it scared me. So I sort of freaked out."

The psychologist nodded. "Mmm-hmm. And the second time?"

I thought for a moment. "There was a lot going on. A car

crash, kids screaming, power poles dropping—but after I froze the fire hydrant's water, I remember feeling good. Like I made a difference by saving those kids?"

"Do you *like* to help people?" Mr. Gillespie asked.

"I guess." And since Spencer was watching me, I added, "And I like helping animals, too."

Spencer wagged his tail approvingly.

Mr. Gillespie wheeled back to his computer. As he typed, he mumbled quietly to himself: *"—anxiety combined with wishful thinking—"*

After a few moments, he looked up. "You have a good heart, Noah. And you want to be helpful. So is it possible that you came up with the idea of this special device that helps you *be* helpful? Maybe what we're dealing with here is what I'm going to call ASHD."

"ASHD?" I said doubtfully.

Outside, the flock of California gulls suddenly rose together and flew over the roof of the school.

Inside, Mr. Gillespie seemed pleased with himself. "Yes, yes, 'Altruism Surplus Hyperimaginative Disorder.' Tell me, Noah, have you ever used your magic device for anything else? For instance, do you use it to fly?"

Sheesh! "Why does everyone ask—"

CRACK!

I jumped at the loud sound and turned to the office window—the now-*cracked* office window.

"What was that?" I asked.

Mr. Gillespie was surprised too, but he tried to smile reassuringly. "One of the gulls must have flown into it."

I looked at the window. There was no impact point on it. And there were no feathers stuck to the glass.

CRACK!

Another big crack appeared in the office window, crisscrossing the first—and at the same time, the office walls shuddered a little.

Spencer calmly scratched his ear.

"I don't think that was a bird," I said, my voice shaking a little.

Mr. Gillespie shook his head. As he did, his helmet-hair didn't move at all.

Meep-meep-meep!

The fire alarm! Outside Mr. Gillespie's room, bright lights started flashing throughout the school office. But it didn't make any sense: How could a *fire* break a window?

Then I got an idea. "Hey, is this an—"

SMASH!

This time, the cracked office window shattered inward, showering Mr. Gillespie, Spencer, and me with bits of broken glass.

"*Earthquake!*" Mr. Gillespie yelled, throwing himself under his desk.

I already knew that California had lots of earthquakes, but

I'd never been *in* one. Still, our school practiced earthquake drills all the time. These started with hiding under a desk and ended with the whole class parading outside.

As I looked around for another desk, the office walls swayed, and crashing sounds came from near and far. I could hear high-pitched screaming and teachers shouting.

As for Spencer, he finally stood up from his cushion and gave me an accusing look that seemed to say, *What did you do now, fool?*

20

"MR. GILLESPIE? SIR?"

The school psychologist was covering his face with his hands. Also, his foot was on my chest. But that wasn't really his fault. Even as short as he was, there was barely enough room under his desk for all three of us.

Spencer tried licking Mr. Gillespie's face to calm him down, but it didn't seem to help. Still, you can't blame a therapy dog for trying.

Meep-meep-meep!

Warm air poured in through the broken office window. Then the floor beneath us shuddered again. I think I would have been more scared if Mr. Gillespie wasn't having a nervous breakdown. But his terror didn't leave any room under the desk for me to be frightened, too.

"Mr. Gillespie . . . are you okay?"

"Okay, okay, okay," Mr. Gillespie chanted, hugging his knees and rocking back and forth.

Spencer looked at me and almost shrugged. *Hey, I didn't pick my owner,* he seemed to say.

"We should probably stay put," I said reassuringly.

"Stay put, stay put," he mumbled.

Spencer didn't disagree.

But now we heard a new noise over the fire alarm. It was a distant rumbling, almost like the sea was rushing in at high tide. But that *couldn't* be right—we were twenty miles from the ocean! The mysterious rumbling was getting louder. *What is that?* It lured me out of the cramped safety of the desk. I peeked my head up, looked out the broken window, and saw—

What is THAT?

A large swell was coming through the parking lot, just like an ocean wave before it hits shore. This earth-swell moved fast, crumbling the parking lot pavement and lifting up cars, then dropping them down out of sight behind it as the swell moved.

The solid earth was acting like water—it was like the ground was doing a pop-and-lock! I stared as the earth-swell hit the lawn in front of the school. Now it became a *green* wave, pushing up the grass into a long, horizontal hill that stretched to my left and right, coming closer. . . .

And now it was almost to Mr. Gillespie's office and—*yikes!*

I jerked my head back under the desk. As I did, the ripple passed under us, lifting the floor up a couple of feet, then passing beneath us to the wall and then into the office beyond.

Walls crunched! Bookshelves toppled! Broken glass and dust blew everywhere! Mr. Gillespie screamed! I screamed! And Spencer sort of yipped.

Meep-meep-me—

At least the fire alarm finally stopped.

And then it was quiet. Although there was still a crash here and there—probably from falling ceilings or furniture—it seemed like the earthquake was over.

From a distance, I heard a teacher's voice. "Students, the only way out is through the windows!" Then the happy cheers of kids breaking glass rang out. A moment later, small groups of third graders ran across the school's front lawn. Some kids were even laughing and chasing each other, like this was a surprise holiday.

Mr. Gillespie was coming back to his senses. He took his thumb out of his mouth and said, "Now where were we, Noah? Oh, yes—ASHD."

I held my finger to my lips. "Listen."

Mr. Gillespie was quiet. We listened.

"Do you hear that?" I asked.

Spencer whined uneasily.

It sounded like more screaming.

* * *

Swirling dust rushed in the room when I opened Mr. Gillespie's office door. I slammed the door shut again. As Spencer came out from under the desk and nuzzled my hand, I got an idea.

"Can I borrow this?" I asked, untying the pink bandanna from Spencer's neck.

Spencer gratefully licked my face. *Dog breath!*

I refolded the bandanna and tied it around my face. Sure, it stank like a dog, and yes, I looked like a stagecoach bandit. But it would help filter the dust out of the air.

I opened the door again and plunged into the dust. From under his desk, Mr. Gillespie squeaked, "Good talk, Noah. Let's continue it later."

Through the clouds of debris, I saw the school office was turned upside down. Parts of the floor had buckled. Shelves were knocked off their walls. Broken lights flickered and dangled from the ceiling.

It was eerie.

Eerie and deserted—there wasn't a single student or teacher in sight. *I guess all of our earthquake drills finally paid off!* I went through the office to the hallway. It was quiet out there, too. So quiet I could hear footsteps approaching. And as the footsteps got louder, I started to get kind of spooked.

"W-who's there?"

Out of the misty, powdery dust, a chunky, dark-haired kid appeared. Spotting me, he stopped in his tracks and threw his hands over this head.

Huh?

As I got closer, something about this kid seemed familiar—he was wearing dress pants.

"Ronnie?" I asked. "What are you doing?"

"N-Noah?" Ronnie Ramirez slowly dropped his arms. "You scared me with that m-mask—I thought you were a robber."

I shook my head in disbelief. "It's a good thing you surrendered," I said. "The first thing most robbers do after an earthquake is loot the closest school."

Ronnie just looked at me. (He doesn't have a very good sense of humor.)

"Ronnie, *what are you doing*?" I repeated.

He looked around. "We were in B-Band. I was in the middle of playing my t-tuba solo. Then the ground shook, and even though I wasn't d-done, Mrs. Ernst ran out of the room. And ev-everyone followed her."

I waited, but that seemed to be the end of the story. "And?"

Ronnie Ramirez shrugged. "And I-I waited a while, but no one came back. So now I'm just sort of sn-snooping around. School is d-dismissed, right?"

"Yeah, definitely. There's hardly anybody left in the office," I said. "Come on, I'll go out with you." The two of us started for the school's front exit. We had to pick our way carefully because the school's trophy case had exploded and there were toppled awards *everywhere*.

Going down the hallway, we saw every classroom door was

wide open. *That's a good sign,* I thought. *The teachers stayed cool-headed and evacuated their classes—*

But then I heard the screaming again. It was clearer now, and coming from the eighth-grade hallway, where the dust was the thickest.

"HAAAAALP!"

"Why don't you go ahead, Ronnie," I said, pushing him to the exit. "I'm right behind you." Ronnie stumbled to the front door, which I knew would lock behind him. Then I turned and headed for the eighth-grade hallway.

It was REALLY dusty, but I didn't have to stumble far. I could hear the screams coming from a closed classroom door on my right. Waving my hand to clear the air revealed piles of ceiling tile in front of a closed door. And above, poking down through the ceiling and wedged against the door, was a big steel strut.

This must've been a roof brace that the earthquake had knocked loose. And since the classroom door opened *out* into the hallway, the eighth-grade class was trapped inside.

I turned the doorknob and pulled. But it didn't budge.

"Let us out!" There was that voice again, the one that had been screaming. It sounded like a boy.

"The door is blocked!" I yelled back.

A brassy girl's voice answered. "We know, Einstein!"

I thought of the third graders who'd broken out of their classroom. "Why don't you just go out the windows?"

"The windows are blocked too, you @#!&$!" the girl shouted.

Well, that *wasn't very nice.*

Unsure of what to do next, I yelled, "What class is this, anyway?"

"Homework Lab. You know, like Study Hall?" answered the girl. There was a pause. "Why do you care? Do you need to evacuate the *real* classes first?"

Sheesh! "No, I was just wond—"

A boy's voice cut in. "Mr. Torpor left right before the quake hit. Now hurry up and get help—we're running out of air!"

So there was no adult, no air, and no exit.

These kids needed help. And that meant I needed the quincunx—*now!*

21

Mrs. Sanchez's room was totally destroyed. The windows were broken out, parts of the ceiling had fallen down, and all the desks were upended.

I picked my way through the rubble, carefully stepping over the broken beakers that'd been hurled to the floor—and that's when I saw her, facedown in a pile of student lab folders. I ran over, grabbed Mrs. Sanchez's shoulder, and rolled her over. I gasped. She had a gigantic red bruise on her temple. She must have fallen and smashed her head against a lab table.

I reached for her wrist to feel a pulse—but I couldn't feel anything! "Mrs. Sanchez?" I pleaded. "Mrs. Sanchez!"

Nothing. My science teacher was gone. Departed. DEAD.

I gently set her hand back down. *This is so unfair! Why couldn't it have been my PE teacher?*

Outside the broken windows, the California gulls had

returned to the trash can, cawing and cackling. I turned back to my fallen science teacher, my eyes misty.

"Why her?" I wailed. "Why?"

"Noah?" Mrs. Sanchez whispered. Her brown eyes fluttered open. "Why are you wearing Spencer's bandana?"

I quickly blinked away my tears. "You're not dead!"

"If you say so." She tried to sit up, grimaced, and brought a hand up to her bruised temple. "But I feel like I *should* be," she moaned, lying back down.

With Mrs. Sanchez alive, I remembered why I was there in the first place.

I quickly made my way to her desk. The earthquake had knocked a display case of rodent skeletons onto it. But as I carefully picked through glass and bleached gopher bones, a familiar round disc glittered green and purple.

The quincunx.

I carefully brushed it off and started for the door. But then I stopped and walked back to my fallen science teacher.

"Mrs. Sanchez," I said, "I need to try to save some suffocating eighth graders."

Mrs. Sanchez nodded weakly. "Noah," she said, "be *very* careful."

"I will," I promised. "Of course, it might be dangerous, but I'm their only hope."

"No," she said. "I meant *be very careful with the quincunx.* It's a major scientific discovery!"

"Oh."

"I'm back!" I yelled at the blocked door. "Don't worry. You'll be out of there before you suffocate!"

"Yay!" the girl called sarcastically. (She sure didn't sound like she was getting weaker.) "How're you going to save us, anyway?"

"Um, we have a team out here working on it!" This, of course, was a lie.

And at that moment, the school shook again. Suddenly I found myself on the floor as a series of groans and crashes came from up and down the hallway. Lockers crumpled like shrieking soda cans. Doors popped open, spewing out books, stuffed animals, backpacks, and lunches. The screams of the trapped eighth graders filled the air.

After the ground stopped shaking, the air was thick with dust again. I stood and slipped into the adjacent classroom. The air there was easier to breathe, but it was very dark.

I pulled the quincunx out and pushed the stem. Green light spilled into the gloom. I worked my way to the bank of windows high on the far wall, stood on a desk, and pried one open. As the window swung in, it revealed a cheap-looking plywood wall on the other side.

No exit.

I figured out what'd happened. See, portable classrooms were perched on a small rise behind the eighth-grade wing. The earthquake must have popped a portable off its footing, making it slide downhill, right up against *these* classroom windows.

"Noah?" called a voice behind me. A figure swayed in the doorway. *Mrs. Sanchez!* "More aftershocks are coming," she said. "We need to get everyone out of here quickly."

I peered through the dust. "Aftershocks?"

Mrs. Sanchez woozily stepped in and sat at a desk. "Aftershocks always follow a big quake."

And now another scream from next door: "I can't breathe!"

So what were our choices? On one hand, Mr. Torpor was probably coming back to rescue his class. But on the other hand, right now the students were terrified and needed help. Yet on the *other* other hand, a team of real firemen should be arriving any second—and I did not want to be using the quincunx when they did.

(And yes, I realize that I just counted three hands.)

A thought occurred to me: *If the earthquake hit the whole city—or state!—it could be HOURS before anyone shows up to help.*

And at that moment, a shock jolted the classroom and more dust rose in the air. Staggered, I half-jumped and half-fell off to the floor. I held the quincunx close to my face and could barely make out a few dark menu choices: CARPAL TUNNEL . . . SUBLEVATION . . . TRANSLOCATE . . .

Of course these don't make any sense!

Speaking to the quincunx, I said, "I'm going with my gut feeling—so don't make me sorry for trusting you." I made my choice and pushed the quincunx stem. Its oval screen flashed brightly in the haze:

CARPAL TUNNEL

CARPAL TUNNEL

CARPAL TUNNEL

Whatever this is, please let it be better than ICK. *Come on, come on.*

Holding the quincunx in that dark, cloudy classroom, a powerful feeling ran through me. I walked to the whiteboard and pictured the trapped students on the other side of the wall.

Pressing my ear against it, I could hear a boy's deep, mournful voice: "I don't think anyone's going to help us. Face it, everyone—we're history."

I needed to DO something—fast!

My hands felt odd. I cracked my knuckles and started drumming my fingers against the whiteboard. The sound was weirdly satisfying. At first, it was a gentle tapping, and then it sounded more like a series of little hammers hitting the hard plastic. Tapping a little harder, the whole whiteboard started shaking—and my hands felt like they were made of steel.

I slowly straightened my fingers out, like I was going to karate chop something. And then I thrust my hand—fingers first—right at the whiteboard.

My fingers broke through the plastic, all the way to the first knuckle. I froze.

Whoa.

Slowly I pulled my hand out of the hole. My fingers were covered in splinters and powder—but as I flexed them, nothing seemed broken, bruised, or even scratched.

So *this* was CARPAL TUNNEL!

I tried hitting the board a little harder this time. It punched right through it, as if the wall were made of Styrofoam. I switched off with my left hand—*bam, BOP, bam, BOP.*

I can bore a hole through the wall! My fists were like jackhammers, tunneling deeper, scooping out shattered whiteboard and broken drywall, making the hole bigger and bigger—

"Noah!" Mrs. Sanchez called from her seat. "I don't think—"

Light-headed with power, I yelled, "They need our help!" And then I got back to jackhammering with my fists and pulling big chunks of splintered wood from the wall.

Mrs. Sanchez stood up unsteadily. "Stop!"

Of course, all teachers hate to see school property destroyed. But what was more important: saving a wall or saving a *life*?

So for the first time ever I ignored a teacher and kept scooping the wall out with my steely fingers. My fists burrowed into the wall like a sapsucker's beak into a tree. And finally, I reached deep and there was a *pop* as my hand went all the way through to the other side.

Success!

Peeking through the hole, I could see dimly lit shapes in the gloom. They were lighting the class with their smartphones—and I could see their outlines creeping forward, anxious to escape their prison. Classroom. Whatever.

"Help's on the way," I called. The cell phones' light revealed that a post in the wall was blocking one side of my hole.

With blow after blow, I karate-chopped chunks of wood off it, and as the splinters flew, the post disappeared. Now the hole was almost big enough for someone to escape through.

Just one more punch should do it. I reared back and cocked my hand behind my head.

"Noah!" Mrs. Sanchez's voice raised. "Listen—"

I didn't listen. Like Thor throwing his hammer, I stepped forward and smashed my hand into the last remaining chunk of post. There was a loud *CRACK* as it broke—and an ominous creak from above.

Backing up, I saw the entire classroom roof lurch down! Sections of ceiling broke off, falling to the floor. And from the frightened curses coming through the hole, the same thing was happening in the other classroom.

"Duck and cover!" shouted Mrs. Sanchez.

I dove under a desk, but after a moment, the roof stopped groaning. Luckily, the hole in the wall didn't cave in, either. Peering through it, I saw the eighth graders were now cowering under their desks.

"Everyone okay?" I called.

"Are you TRYING to kill us?"

"No," I said, "I'm just trying to—"

"Squish us?" jeered another voice. Angrier muttering sprang up, and then a whole classroom of kids' voices joined together.

They were booing me!

22

MRS. SANCHEZ COUGHED. "NOAH, THAT'S A *LOAD-BEARING* wall." She pointed upward. "That means it supports the weight of the building. And you can't just punch through a load-bearing wall without problems."

I sighed and climbed out from under the desk. Using the quincunx was like trying to solve a Rubik's Cube. As soon as I solved one problem, I just made things worse somewhere else.

I brought my hand up to my chest. "I'm sorry for not listening. My fault."

Then I tapped my chest. Something that felt like a tiny runaway train hit me and sent me flying backward.

It was my finger!

Mrs. Sanchez helped me up. "I'm the one who owes *you* an apology, Noah," she said. "You were obviously telling the truth about the quincunx. It's clear that device is not of terrestrial origin—and I should never have sent you to Mr. Gillespie." She paused. "But from a scientific viewpoint, I'm curious about something important."

Finally! A smart grown-up is going to get to the heart of the quincunx's mystery.

"Have you ever used it to fly?" she asked.

I groaned. The drooping ceiling did too, slumping even farther downward. It could collapse any second.

I started toward the hole, but Mrs. Sanchez stepped in front of me. "*You* stay put." Then she turned to the hole and firmly called out. "Students! I know it's dark. I know you're frightened. But please line up and come through this hole one at a time and *very* quickly."

Before Mrs. Sanchez was done talking, a student tumbled through the hole.

Coby Cage.

He peered through the darkness, saw me, and did a double take. "Noah, is that you?" Looking around the ruined classroom, he laughed. "And you thought *I* was going to do something bad with your little toy?" Coby asked incredulously. "*You* just wrecked the school! What were you doing with it, playing Jenga?"

Meanwhile, more confused and coughing eighth graders streamed through the hole behind Coby.

"Go out the door and turn right to the exit," Mrs. Sanchez directed. "Then leave the building just as you would during a normal earthquake drill. I know you've been through a lot, but you'll be safe soon. Let's move more quickly, people!"

Students staggered into the hallway. "Coby, that means you too," said Mrs. Sanchez. Coby gave me a venomous look, then followed his classmates.

Fetching the quincunx from the desk, I pressed its stem. With the connection to CARPAL TUNNEL cut, my hands immediately felt like . . . well, *hands* again.

"Mrs. Sanchez, what does 'carpal' mean?" I asked.

Waving students to the classroom exit, she said, "That relates to the *carpus,* the bones of the wrist, hand, and fingers."

Oh. So the quincunx let me tunnel with my carpals. I ran my fingers over its gleaming surface. *And even though I messed up, the quincunx pretty much just saved the day.*

Mrs. Sanchez came closer and touched my arm. "Noah—again, I want to say that I'm sorry for my behavior. It was wrong for me to confiscate that quincunx."

Hearing a teacher apologize to me was such a new experience, and all I could say was, "Um, that's okay."

She looked me in the eyes. "I always knew you were thoughtful. But, Noah, you're resourceful as well. This quincunx is a complete mystery, but you *are* the expert on it. And I can't think of a better person to be its custodian while we try to discover the truth behind—"

"*Gaaah,*" moaned a voice. "*My nose!*"

The last two kids had ducked through the wall—a really

tall kid being assisted by a stocky girl. The girl was guiding him because he was busy clutching his face. I recognized him—Todd Coulton, the star player on the basketball team.

The girl spotted us. "Whose idea was it to save us by breaking down the wall?" Her voice was familiar—she was the girl I'd been talking to.

"Right here." I smiled, still basking in Mrs. Sanchez's praise. "But there's no need to thank me—"

"Birdbrain!" she yelled. "When the ceiling gave way, something fell on Todd's nose!"

"*Gaaah!*" agreed Todd, with a yelp of pain.

"Sorry," I retorted. "I was just, you know, trying to *save your lives.*"

The girl let go of Todd and put her hands on her hips. Todd started windmilling his arms to keep from falling. "How did *you* save our lives? And who *are* you anyway?"

I realized then that I was still wearing Spencer's pink bandanna.

The girl pointed at the gaping hole in the wall. "And how'd you do *that?*"

"*Gaaah!*" added Todd. (He was a man of few words.)

I pointed to Mrs. Sanchez. "She'll answer all your questions," I said. "But right now, we have to get out of this building fast. It could blow at any second!"

I added that part about the building exploding because it gave me a good excuse to sprint away.

* * *

Seconds later, I was in the school parking lot—or what was left of it. The earthquake had turned the whole thing into a wavy, buckled field of asphalt. And it was swarming with worried parents driving their Subarus like roller-coaster cars over the asphalt hills.

Fire trucks were in front of the school, and somewhere I could hear a woman loudly saying, "This is Rayla Rafferty, LIVE at the scene—"

As I stared at all the kids and parents, a familiar white hybrid screeched to a stop. My parents exploded out of it and sprinted toward me.

"Noah!" cried Mom.

"Thank goodness!" said Dad. Then the three of us wrapped our arms around one another in a group hug.

I know that everyone's parents talk about "love" and how they'll "always be there" for their kids. But I never really got what that meant until right then, as we stood there in the destroyed parking lot, hugging and swaying.

If something bad happened to me, my parents really *would* be there. They loved me—and I loved them back.

As I looked over Mom's shoulder, I noticed something across the parking lot. Four younger kids, grouped together on their bikes. *Are they going to ride on the earthquake hills?* I wondered. But no, they were just sitting there, staring at us. They looked . . . familiar.

In the front of the group was a plump boy on a bright-orange bike. *That's the same kid who went flying out of the bathroom stall.* And seeing him back on that bike reminded me where I'd seen him before that. It was back when the power pole broke in front of the Brights' house!

"Let's get you home," Dad said, holding the front passenger door open. Getting in, I looked out the window and saw the orange-bike kid hand something to one of the others before they pedaled off together.

"We were SO worried," said Mom, driving up a rise of asphalt. "All the school phone lines were down, so we had no way of contacting you!" She swerved around an overturned school bus.

A crossing guard in a bright-green vest stood in the parking lot's driveway. She scolded two girls jaywalking across the street, then made us wait as a white ambulance flew by, its siren howling.

"They're never going to sell any ice cream going *that* fast," said Dad. (It's his favorite joke.)

Mom looked over at me. "We want to hear everything. But first, are you okay, honey?"

"I'm okay."

"But that quake must have been terrifying," said Dad. "Are you *really* okay?"

"I'm okay."

Mom smiled at me. "Is it okay that we keep asking if you're okay?"

"It's okay."

As Mom pulled out onto the road, I was surprised to see that its surface was still smooth. *Why isn't the street wrecked like the parking lot?*

"Hang on," said Mom, pulling over and stopping as three police cars went screaming past. Then she turned to me with a grave expression. "Since we have a minute, there *is* something serious your father wants to ask you about."

"Dead serious," said Dad from behind.

They know about the quincunx. I gulped, touched my scar, and reached a decision: *I'm just going to tell them everything.*

"Son," Dad said, "what happened to my peanut butter?"

23

<u>The Robert F. Moral School Newsletter</u>
Principal's Message

Dear Parents, Students, and Friends,

What a week!

Every school year has moments of comedy, drama, and tragedy. But since when do all three strike at the same moment? Yet that's exactly what happened this week, when R.F.M. School was hit by its very own earthquake!

Thanks to good emergency preparedness, all of our students and staff got through the ordeal safely. And it really was our ordeal. The state's seismologist has analyzed the data, and she believes our school was the epicenter of a very small but very intense earthquake. Luckily, this isolated earthquake—and its aftershocks—left most of the rest of our Santa Rosa community untouched.

Let me express my most enthusiastic gratitude to the students and staff. None of us has ever experienced a crisis like this before. It would have been easy to panic in the chaos and think only of oneself. But instead, from classroom to classroom, I have heard many tales of heroism. I salute you all!

Everybody has his or her own story to tell, and I'll share some of them in future newsletters. I must say, some of these are almost unbelievable. For example, after the earthquake hit, I understand that Mr. Gillespie took refuge by standing under *his desk.*

Of course, I'm just kidding—Mr. Gillespie isn't really that short! ☺ *But during difficult times, the most important thing we can do is keep smiling. And we need all the smiles we can get! Because while our school is still intact, it suffered a lot of property damage, mostly from falling furniture, lockers, and ceiling tiles.*

The worst of it was in the eighth-grade hall, where a fallen truss and a toppled temporary classroom briefly blocked students from exiting the building.

It really is a miracle that—with two exceptions— nobody was seriously hurt. As you may know, Todd Coulton, the basketball team captain, was injured in the quake. He is recovering at Sutter Hospital. Also, Mr. Torpor was struck by a ream of lavender copy paper and knocked unconscious. Happily, tests revealed no lasting damage. I've always said that teachers have thick skins (and skulls!). ☺

In many ways, this event has brought our school closer together. Right now, cleanup crews are out sweeping the halls, picking up broken glass, and getting things back to normal. There's a lot more work ahead, but we are determined not to let this violent earthquake disrupt the student learning in our community.

Classes will resume on Monday *in the portable classrooms set up on the school's upper playground. So I guess you could say the "moral high ground" is always there when you need it.* ☺

I'll have more updates as our school cleanup and reconstruction continues. But for now, let's all keep on keeping calm—and carrying on.

All the best,
Bruce Lapinski
Principal, Robert F. Moral School

24

The day after the earthquake, I was up to my neck in water.

See, school was cancelled for the rest of the week. So the Brights had invited my family over for a late afternoon Aftershock Barbecue. And since it was still totally hot, I'd jumped in the pool to cool off.

Standing on my tiptoes, the water was just below my chin, but the sun was still baking my face. *Dang, how hot* is *it?* I tried to read the outdoor thermometer on the side of the house, but the glare made it impossible. Raising a hand to block the sun, I lost my balance and had to step backward, toward the deep end. So my outstretched foot met—nothing?

I plunged underwater, swallowing a mouthful of pool water in the process. Floundering toward the shallow end, I gasped and coughed, then paddled to the side.

"Hey, Noah," Jason called out from the patio. "Be careful not to get in over your head."

"Thanks, but too late." At least now I could see the thermometer: 104 degrees.

Mr. Bright and my parents were talking over at the grill, and the smell of hot dogs filled the air. Crawling over the pool's edge, I hotfooted it across the baking concrete and sat on a wooden chair next to Jenny and Jason. My wet bathing suit stuck to the warm wooden slats.

Of course, I'd already told the twins most of my not-so-amazing story.

Jenny spread more sunscreen on her arms and picked up the story. "So after you got everyone out, that girl *dissed* you?"

"Yep," I said, sipping some iced lemonade. "She wasn't grateful at all."

"Haven't you heard?" asked Jason, trying to imitate his sister. "A good deed is its *own* reward." Taking off his mirrored sunglasses, he gave us a secretive look. "Listen, I've been cooking up something important. Something *big*."

He waved for us to get closer.

We got closer.

"Yeah?" said Jenny.

"What is it?" I asked.

Jason leaned to one side. What happened next was *so* loud, it sounded like someone had torn a sheet of plywood in half.

While Jenny and I laughed in disgusted awe at his gaseous explosion, Jason sat proudly back in his chair.

"Look out for aftershocks."

"JASON!" Mr. Bright was outraged. "THESE ARE OUR GUESTS."

"Sorry, everyone," Jason called. (He totally didn't mean it.)

Jenny waved her hand in front of her face. "What will it take for you to be a mature, responsible person?"

"Dunno," shrugged Jason. "Reincarnation?" He turned to me. "Hey, Noah, speaking of earthquakes, think about this. The first time you used the quincunx, that power pole fell in front of our house. Then yesterday you had it with you—"

"And there was an earthquake that only affected *our* school," added Jenny. "Suspicious much? Seriously, I'm just waiting for the next domino to fall."

I gave her a look. "Yeah, but the power pole fell because of woodpecker holes or something. And the earthquake was caused by . . . movements in the earth's crust. Right?" The twins just looked at me. "Seriously, you think those things are connected to the quincunx?"

Jenny confirmed the hypothesis: "Duh!"

I jumped as Mr. Bright called over to us. "HAVE ANY OF YOU SEEN WHAT'S GOING ON AT NOYD WOODS?"

The black swifts! "The earthquake didn't cause any damage there, did it?" I asked.

"No, it wasn't affected," Mom answered. "But there *is* construction going on near that waterfall."

"No, that's impossible," I said. "It's a nature preserve."

"Actually, it's private property, owned by the Noyd family," said Dad. "They've just called it a 'nature preserve' all these years."

"That's a rip-off! I mean, what makes something a nature preserve?" Jenny asked. "Isn't there *nature* there that needs *preserving*?"

"GOOD POINT, HONEY," said Mr. Bright. "NOW, WHO'S HUNGRY?"

I wasn't. I had a plan, and I needed to get to Noyd Woods like, right away. But first, I needed a disguise.

"Jason," I said. "Can I borrow a hoodie?"

"Sure, why not?" he answered. "It's only a thousand degrees out."

25

WELCOME TO THE FUTURE HOME
OF CATARACT GROVE

I slammed on my brakes and skidded to a halt. In front of me loomed a sign that was so big, it blocked the trailhead up to Noyd Falls.

Two bulldozers sat parked next to it.

Cataract Grove? That name rang a bell . . . and then I remembered. After Coby ambushed me at the bus stop, I'd run into wires holding a sign for Cataract Grove.

Jason pulled up next to me on his bike. "You've *got* to be kidding me."

The sign showed a sprawling new house surrounded by trees. In the front yard, adults waved merrily as kids played catch with a football. And in the imaginary house's backyard was . . . a *waterfall.*

My blood ran cold.

In the distance, I heard the deep rumble of an engine. Jason looked back, hopped off his bike, pushed it behind the sign, then started sprinting up the trail. "Come on!"

I quickly hid my bike too, then looked around. "Jason?"

"Psst! Over here!" Jason hissed from a patch of tall grass. I walked over, and he pulled me down next to him.

"What's going on?"

"Look!" Jason pointed down to the road just as a pickup roared into view. The truck was black, with flames painted on the hood and the sides of the cab. But the flames weren't yellow or red—instead they were camouflage flames, with splotches of green and brown and gray.

"You're afraid of camo?" I asked. Jason glared at me. "Wait, I get it. It's dumb to make the flames in camouflage, because—"

"Forget the paint job," Jason interrupted. "Look who's behind the wheel."

I looked at the driver. It was Coby Cage! *But how could that be?*

"That's *Brock* Cage," said Jason. "Coby's older brother. He dropped out of high school to become a Mixed Martial Arts fighter." Jason plucked at the bright-green hoodie I was wearing. "Get down! This thing is so bright, he'll spot you from a mile away."

I ducked. "But why would Brock be looking for me?"

Jason sighed. "Look, I didn't want to say anything, but

Ronnie Ramirez texted me. He says that Coby said something to his brother, and now Brock's out for revenge—"

I stood up. This had nothing to do with the black swift. And I was done running away.

"Noah? Hey, what are you doing?"

I was already headed up the trail to the waterfall. Jason easily caught up with me, and a few minutes later, the two of us burst into the little clearing at Noyd Falls.

It had changed since my last visit—a LOT. For one thing, there were wooden stakes pounded all around the canyon floor. Tied around the top of each stake was a bright-red plastic strip.

"Hey, those are survey flags," said Jason. "I remember them from when Dad worked construction, back before Mom—" He stopped, and his lips tightened. "Anyway, these stakes mean someone's already measured out this whole area."

"So Cataract Grove is going to be right *here*?" I clenched my fists. "That means houses will back right up to the waterfall. And the black swift—"

Plik-plik-plik-plik.

I spun toward the falls. And there, almost hidden by the water's spray, the black swift was hanging on a wet rock, watching us.

"Whoa," whispered Jason. "That's the bird who lives behind the waterfall? Awesome."

"I know, right?" A hot breeze swept through the air. The black swift called again.

Plik-plik-plik-plik.

This time, muffled by the waterfall, there was an answering call from behind the falls.

Plik-plik-plik-plik.

"There are two of them," I said.

Jason held up his finger. "Listen!"

Plik-plik-plik-plik.

This third voice was faint and tiny—like a baby's. *A defenseless baby.*

"There's a whole bird family here," Jason said. His smile disappeared, and he looked away. I knew what he was thinking about.

A whole family.

And then I pictured Jason's mom.

MRS. ELLEN BRIGHT *(Cygnus benignus)*

APPEARANCE: Tall. Fit. Ruddy face, dark hair. Big, perfect teeth.

VOICE: Kind words, rich laughter.

PLUMAGE: Unpredictable. One day, she might wear a Pokémon T-shirt and a skirt, the next, an expensive black pantsuit with a colorful scarf.

RANGE: Anywhere you needed her to be.

SOCIAL BEHAVIOR: Always smiling. People flocked to her everywhere she went.

STATUS: Extinct.

I listened to the faint birdcall again.

Plik-plik-plik-plik.

It's almost for sure that the builders behind Cataract Grove didn't want to drive away the black swifts. Most likely, they didn't even *know* about the birds. They were driving and fiddling with the stereo.

Or if the builders did know, they didn't care. They were knocking over dominoes without even watching where they fell. Or knowing they existed.

It was just so *stupid*—

"Noah?" Jason was snapping his fingers in my face and looking concerned. "Noah! Take it easy." He pointed at my arm. I'd been scratching angrily at my scar through the hoodie. Pushing the sleeve up, I could see it was now a bright-red, angry seam.

"Is that blood?!" Jason asked. "You got *blood* on my best hoodie?"

"It's not blood," I said dully.

Jason crossed his arms. "Okay, so what *is* it, then?"

I looked down. "Oh, that. Yeah, it's blood."

Jason rolled his eyes. "It's okay, you just made a rash decision." He forced a laugh. "Get it? A *rash* decision!"

I really wanted to tell Jason what I'd been thinking about,

but why remind my best friend that his mom was dead?[6]

Jason glanced up. The sun was pale and starting to set behind the trees. "It's getting dark. Let's come back tomorrow—"

"No way!" I said. "This could all be *bulldozed* tomorrow. We have to do something about this now."

6. FIELD NOTES: My Scar

In the last minute of her life, Mrs. Bright was carrying a cloth shopping bag filled with veggies and a carton of milk. Her hair was pulled back with a polka-dotted headband.

Walking on Mrs. Bright's right was Jenny. And on her other side was me. I'd gone to the Brights' house that day to see Jason, but his soccer practice was running late, so Mrs. Bright asked if I wanted to walk up to the corner store while I waited.

She was good at including people, and I liked being included. As we walked back home, Mrs. Bright turned to look at me over her shoulder. "Noah?" she asked. "Do you know the name of a water bird with a big white patch behind its eyes?"

"Probably a bufflehead," I answered. But before I could ask where she'd seen one, something big hit the curb behind us. Mrs. Bright's eyes widened—the sound of an engine was suddenly much too loud, too close. There was no time to turn, no time to yell a warning. Mrs. Bright just reached out with both arms and shoved Jenny to one side and me to the other.

I later learned that a red SUV had swerved off the street, driven up on the sidewalk, and hit Mrs. Bright from behind. The doctors said she died instantly. (The doctors always say that.)

Jenny was spun to the side, into someone's yard. As the SUV drove over her, Jenny was pressed deep into the lawn. She was knocked out, and her spinal injuries put her in a wheelchair.

The side of the car just clipped me, and I flew through the air. I mean, I really *flew*, like I'd been shot from a cannon. Coming down in the street, I tried to break my fall with a hand. Instead, I broke my forearm in three places. The red SUV had stopped, shielding Jenny and Mrs. Bright from me. All I could see was a canvas shopping bag leaking milk into the gutter.

Later, surgeons put my bones back together with metal plates. And sure, I got a nasty scar—but I got off easy. So did the SUV driver. He didn't get behind the wheel that day intending to kill someone. No. He was just a guy adjusting his stereo, not paying attention to where he was going. In court, the driver testified that he'd never even seen us. Without even looking up, he'd devastated the Bright family forever.

"Totally," agreed Jason. "Listen, let's play paintball near the Cataract Grove billboard. Who knows? Maybe we'll 'accidentally' hit it over and over. And you can write some clever signs for us to put on the trees. You know, something like, *'Whoever chops me down will suffer greatly.'* Okay?"

"Great ideas," I said, nodding—but I had a very different plan in mind. "You know what, why don't you go ahead, Jason? I'll catch up with you later."

His eyes narrowed. "Hey, you're not going to do something crazy up here, are you?"

I held up my hands in surrender. "When do *I* ever get crazy? And don't worry, if it gets dark, I'll use your green hoodie to light the way." I looked at its sleeve. "Sorry about the blood."

"I don't really care about that," he said. This was probably a lie, but it was a nice lie. "All right. Later."

We fist-bumped, Jason took off, and I went and sat on a rock. I needed to wait for darkness. Water splashed, birds rustled in the forest, and after a long while, twilight deepened.

I'm a birder, so I'm good at being patient. But as I waited, time passed more slowly than ketchup dripping from a bottle. Finally, the sky turned a deep violet. Stars started popping out here and there.

Plik-plik-plik-plik, called the baby black swift. I imagined the little bird staring out at the flowing wall of water in its front yard. *Did it dream of the world beyond the waterfall?*

Staring up at the stars, I thought of my first plane trip. I was six. My parents and I were on a night flight to Georgia for a job. At thirty-five thousand feet, I'd pressed my nose against the window and looked out at the constellations of house and town and city lights far below.

I'm way up here, but people are living their lives way *down there.*

It was an amazing feeling.

Looking up at the constellations above Noyd Woods, I had that same sense of wonder. But now it was mixed with anger. *I'm in the middle of an infinite universe. But in that whole vast space, there's only* one *species called the black swift. It's a precious, amazing animal . . . but people just live their own lives without noticing anything else. So nobody cares about the black swift at all.*

Nobody but me.

26

It was time to begin.

I pulled the quincunx out of my pocket and looked up at the stars again. *Maybe there's someone out there, a thousand light-years away, with a quincunx just like this one.*

Pulling the lime-green hoodie over my head, I tied the drawstrings tight. That would have to do for my disguise. Now I was almost ready for action—but a thought nagged me. Was I "sticking up for what I thought was right" or "doing something crazy"?

Or both?

I felt for the indentations on the back of the quincunx. When I'd put a finger in the center one, a pop-up menu appeared. But what would happen if I put *five* fingertips in all five quincunx holes?

As I tried different fingertip holds, I nearly dropped the disc a couple of times. But I found that if I balanced the quincunx with my thumb in the middle dot, my other four fingers could find the corners.

And with the quincunx perched on my fingertips, two things happened.

1. The screen appeared and turned red.

2. A beautiful song started playing. A beautiful song that was playing in my hand!

The quincunx was *ringing*. And its ringtone was a catchy little tune, like you'd hear on a baby's computer game. It even had words—sweet children's voices singing:

"Greet-ings! You have a mess-age! Oh, greet-ings! Please check your mess-age!"

Okay, so the lyrics weren't that great. I was so stunned that all I did was stare at that red screen. My heart started racing as the song got louder and louder.

"GREET-INGS! Please check your MESS-AGE!"

"You're sort of freaking me out right now," I said to the quincunx.

Could it be? Was this the moment? Was it finally time for all of my questions to be answered?

I took a deep breath and tapped the quincunx's screen—and it turned emerald green as words appeared:

GREETINGS. THIS IS NOAH?

My palms were slick with sweat. There was no keyboard to write back. I held the quincunx up to my face. Very loudly and very slowly, I said, "Yeah. Yes. This is me. I mean, I'm here. You know, Noah. Who is this?"

The green screen's words changed:

I AM [ɒɤ°]

I was so startled, I bobbled the puck. See, when I looked at the "[ɒɤ°]," the quincunx made an odd sound, like a seal trying not to giggle.

"Um, I'm not sure I can pronounce your name?" I found that looking at the strange symbols triggered the stifled seal giggle again.

VERY WELL, the screen flashed. I BELIEVE A CORRESPOND-ING VERSION OF MY NAME IN YOUR LANGUAGE WOULD BE . . . ZORCHA T'WIRPO.

"Oh, come on," I said. "Seriously?" There was an awkward silence. "So how's it going . . . Zorcha T'wirpo?"

A new message: IT GOES WELL. THANK YOU FOR THE INQUIRY. YOU MAY REFER TO ME SIMPLY AS "T'WIRPO."

I waited. And at some point, I realized Zorcha T'wirpo wasn't going to add anything else. *I don't know* who *this is,* I told myself. *But this* could *be an alien . . . which means I could be the first human to ever speak with someone from another world. So now's the time to make a good first impression!*

I smoothed my hair down with one hand, adjusted my glasses, and tucked in my T-shirt so it didn't stick out under the hoodie. *That should do it!* "T'wirpo, can I ask where you live?"

YES.

Nothing. "Hello? Still there?"

APOLOGIES FOR THE STRANGENESS OF MY POOR ANSWERS. INTERACTING WITH YOUR SPECIES IS NEW TO ME.

My species?

ALSO, I AM DISTRACTED BY THE FILAMENTS OF DEAD PROTEIN COMING OUT OF YOUR HEAD. DO THEY HURT YOU?

I brushed my hair out of my eyes. "No, not really. I'm supposed to get them cut next week." *So this Zorcha T'wirpo can see me.* "Can you tell me where you're from?"

FAR, FAR AWAY.

I rolled my eyes. "Could you be more specific? Like, are you in this solar system?"

I WAS BORN IN A PLACE SO DISTANT, YOUR SCIENTISTS ARE NOT AWARE OF WHERE MY POO IS.

This was the weirdest conversation I'd ever had. "T'wirpo, why do you think our scientists would care about your *poo*?"

BECAUSE MY POO WOULD TELL YOU SOMETHING ABOUT ME.

The odd thing was, this actually made sense. I mean, biologists study bird poop all the time. So alien poop really *would* give scientists interesting information. (But still!)

A new message winked onto the quincunx screen. APOLOGIES! I AM USING INITIALS FROM YOUR LANGUAGE. "P-O-O" STANDS FOR "PLANET OF ORIGIN."

"Oh!" I said, relieved. "So your *planet of origin* is really far away."

YES. BUT EXTRATERRESTRIAL "POO" WOULD ALSO BE EDUCA-
TIONAL FOR HUMANKIND, I AM SURE.

Great. I was using an intergalactic cell phone to talk to an advanced life form about poo. "T'wirpo, where can I leave this, um, device so that you can get it back?"

YOU CALL IT THE "QUINCUNX," NO? IT IS A FINE NAME. BUT NO, YOU MUST KEEP IT. I GREW THE QUINCUNX FOR YOU.

A picture popped up on the quincunx screen. At first it looked like a blurred photo of a small bush growing in a back-yard garden. But everything about it looked a little . . . different. For example, the bush's branches were heavy with fruit—but the fruit were quincunxes that sparkled and glittered in the light. These discs had different shades; some glittered emerald and purple, like mine; others had iridescent shades of gold and blue and black and—actually, I'm not sure I had even seen some of those colors before.

The rest of the scene seemed pretty normal . . . that is, aside from the four moons in the sky behind the bush. The smallest moon had two rings around it, sort of like an overachieving Saturn.

"Wow," I said. And I meant it!

The picture faded back into the green screen. MY PROJECT WITH YOU MAY END SOON, NOAH. PLEASE CONSIDER THE CHOICES YOU WILL MAKE IN THE MEANTIME.

"Wait, what project?" I asked. "What choices?" But there was no answer, and the quincunx screen went blank, then disappeared entirely.

I guess they don't say "good-bye" on his POO. I ran my finger over the quincunx's bump. *And hey, this really* is *its stem!*

I looked up at the stars and felt like waving. My heart was drumming as fast as a hairy woodpecker drilling into a tree. *I was just talking with—with—what, exactly?*

Whatever it was, T'wirpo had told me to think about the choices I wanted. Okay, fine. I looked around me. Cataract Grove had invaded the nature preserve with its red flags and lumber and bulldozers.

What I want is for all *of that to go away.* I looked at the quincunx. *So am I supposed to just* wish *for it? Or should I use the quincunx . . . ?*

Grayed-out words flashed past as I scrolled through the menu. Here and there, the blur of a word in black darted past: EXPROPRIATE . . . LANIATE . . . WRACK . . .

I had no idea what these words meant. Still, all I had to do was look at the little red ribbons surrounding me to see how much was at stake. So I tried something new—I *thought* about what I wanted. Then I backtracked on the menu, looking for the word that felt right to me.

Got one! Taking a deep breath, I made my choice. *And here we go.*

EXPROPRIATE

EXPROPRIATE

EXPROPRIATE

27

[TV NEWS THEME MUSIC FADES OUT.]

News Anchor Jim Bottoms: Good evening, and welcome to the Eleven O'Clock News on Channel Five. In our top story tonight, Santa Rosa police are looking for clues to a mystery at a local construction site. Rayla Rafferty has more at the scene. Rayla?

[Cut to live remote camera.]

Rayla Rafferty: Jim, I'm here *LIVE* at Noyd Woods. Developers recently purchased the quiet woodland area from the Noyd family—but all plans for the site are currently on hold. That's because earlier tonight, Noyd Woods became the site of a mysterious disappearance. In a Channel Five *exclusive,* Santa Rosa Police Chief Mitch Castleberry tells us more.

Chief Castleberry (blinking in the bright TV lights): Hello.

Rayla Rafferty: Chief, you're *on the air.* Please tell us about this shocking crime!

Chief Castleberry: Well, I don't know if it's shocking. I do know that Noyd Woods was recently divided up into residential building sites. The developers moved in some heavy machinery as well as construction materials—

Rayla Rafferty (impatiently): But then something *horrible* happened?

Chief Castleberry: Well, all of the survey stakes are gone, if that's what you mean.

Rayla Rafferty (turns dramatically to camera): But that's not *all* that's gone, is it, Chief?

Chief Castleberry: No. It also looks like all of the construction materials are missing—including the bulldozers.

Rayla Rafferty: Chief, are there any suspects? A competing construction company? College pranksters? Environmental extremists?

Chief Castleberry (holding up his hand): We have no idea. Right now, we're treating this as a simple case of theft. How the perpetrators did it so quickly and quietly is a puzzle, but we are pursuing some leads—

My hand was shaking as I hit the "mute" button to my bedroom's TV.

The police already *found out? That was fast.*

I ran my fingers through my hair. "It's going to be okay," I said to myself. "There's no way the police can know it's me." Taking a deep breath, I turned the volume back on.

Rayla Rafferty: —the police do have *one* eyewitness. Sharon Shuey was hiking here at Noyd Woods when the disappearances occurred. Sharon, who's this you have with you?

Sharon Shuey (holding a beagle in her arms): This here is my big boy, Tipper. He likes to take evening strolls in Noyd Woods, don't you, boy?

Tipper: *Ah-oo-ga!*

Rayla Rafferty: Isn't he precious. Now, can you describe what you saw tonight?

Sharon Shuey: Tipper and I were headed up the trail when we saw a person in a green hoodie coming downhill, toward us. Of course, I wasn't frightened. Lots of our neighbors hike here. Plus, I had my flashlight, and Tipper has the heart of a lion. Don't you, boy?

Tipper (licks microphone)

Sharon Shuey: It was dark, so I didn't get a good look at him. "Hello," I said, but the person just sort of grunted and scurried down the hill. Then I thought "Now that's suspicious."

Rayla Rafferty: Was it the grunting that aroused your suspicions?

Sharon Shuey: No, it was the *hood* that sent up a warning flag. It was pulled around his face—oh, and the color. It was the most hideous bright green you can imagine.

Rayla Rafferty: Chilling! Who knows what this Green-Hooded Bandit was trying to conceal? Thank you, Sharon. And Jim, I'll have more details on the police investigation into the Noyd Woods Mystery as the story unfolds. Now back to you in the studio.

Tipper: *Ah-oo-ga!*

Anchor Jim Bottoms: Thank you, Rayla, for those shocking developments from Santa Rosa's very own backyard. But how about that Tipper? A beagle with a nose for crime. Speaking of which, an eight-year-old boy in Rincon Valley got a bean stuck up his nose today, and fire crews were called to the scene—

click

My heart pounded as I stared at the TV's blank screen. Sure, I knew that what I'd done was "technically" wrong. I'd used the quincunx to break the law. But T'wirpo—or the quincunx?—had basically encouraged me!

I know, I know. "The alien *made* me do it" is sort of a weak argument. After all, I'd chosen to do what I did. But stopping the construction sure seemed like the right thing to do. If only someone had done that in the wetlands years ago, wood ducks would still be around today.

I mean, isn't it okay to do something slightly *bad* for the much greater *good*?

Besides, right now I had other things to worry about. Like, what kind of "project" had T'wirpo signed me up for without even asking me? And, in a more down-to-earth way, was I going to get caught? Was there any evidence that could link me to Cataract Grove?

I glanced around my room and spotted Jason's lime-green hoodie folded on my desk. *Hide the evidence!* I stuffed the hoodie under my bed.

Standing up, I saw my reflection in the darkened bedroom window. I looked worried. I looked guilty. But what were the odds the police could find me? After all, there was only one witness (two, counting Tipper), and all she'd seen was a grunting kid with a green hoodie.

Plus, it wasn't like a high-tech NCIS team was investigating the case. I mean, our police chief's last name was Castleberry. How good could he be?

"There's no way the police know it's me," I repeated to myself. And just like that, I felt a little better.

There was a knock on my bedroom door.

"Come in," I said.

The door swung open. "Noah?" Mom said shakily. "The police are here. They would like to speak with you."

28

"HI, NOAH. I'M DETECTIVE MARLOWE."

The woman stood up from the living room couch. She was tall, almost as tall as Dad, and dressed in jeans and a black turtleneck. Her police badge hung around her neck on a silver chain.

I could see that another police officer—a man in uniform—was in the kitchen talking to Dad. My father looked pale under the lights.

"—but we're as surprised as *you* are, Officer!" Dad protested, waving his arms around. The police officer watched him warily.

Mom turned to me and put her hand on my shoulder. "Noah, I'll be right over there in the kitchen. Excuse me for a moment, Detective." As Mom left, Detective Marlowe fastened her gaze on me. Her eyes were like black buttons, dark with almost no white.

Through the front window, I saw the lights of three police cars parked in front of our house. I could also see people moving around in the darkness.

Huh? What's going on here?

Detective Marlowe was still watching me. "First, let me apologize," she said. "I'm so sorry to wake you."

I tried to answer, but the words caught in my throat and I coughed instead. My hand crept to my scar.

"Do you need a glass of water?" she asked.

"No," I managed to say. "I'm okay. And I wasn't asleep."

"Oh." The detective cocked her head. "Did I interrupt your homework?"

Not trusting myself to speak, I shook my head.

"Good." She sat down on the couch. "You probably finished it all at school, a smart student like you. Except your school's shut this week, isn't it? With the earthquake and all."

"Right," I agreed. *Was she trying to catch me in a lie already?* "The earthquake. And all."

Stop being paranoid. This might not have anything to do with what happened at Noyd Falls.

"The reason I'm here is because of what happened at Noyd Falls."

I started coughing again, and thought back to a few hours before.

* * *

A Few Hours Before

EXPROPRIATE

EXPROPRIATE

EXPROPRIATE

I made my selection, then stared at the silvery waterfall and waited in the darkness. As I waited, I began getting a familiar yet odd feeling in my hands. See, I already knew what it was like to suck a Coke through a straw . . . but now my *palms* were getting that "sucking" sensation!

As I looked at the closest survey stake, I cautiously brought my arm up. Then I opened my fingers, and held my palm out at the red-ribboned stake.

Here goes nothing, I thought, trying to channel EXPROPRIATE to my hand.

But instead of a ray of power shooting *from* my hand *to* the survey stake, the opposite happened. The stake lifted up and out of the ground—and in a flash, it zipped right at *me*. I closed my hand and turned away, but it was too late. The stake somehow disappeared straight *into* my palm. It was gone.

I examined my fist. It looked normal. Slowly and carefully, I opened my fingers. Everything *seemed* okay . . . but my hand still had that same sucking feeling. So I aimed it at another stake—

Flash—zip. Now that stake was gone, too.

If Jason had been there, he'd say, "I always knew you sucked."

So EXPROPRIATE *means "subtract,"* I thought, subtracting every survey stake I could find. *I wonder if it works on bigger things—like bulldozers.*

* * *

Detective Marlowe was still talking: "—your parents told us that you went to Noyd Woods this afternoon. Did you see anything unusual while you were there?"

I shook my head innocently. "Sorry."

"So just to clarify, you didn't see anything unusual?" Detective Marlowe leaned forward to peer a little more closely at me. Her badge dangled in the air. "Nothing at all?"

She knows something's not right. Maybe I should I mention the black swift? It is unusual. . . .

"Well, I did see my neighbor, Mrs. Shuey," I confessed. "And Tipper, her beagle. But that was about it."

"Oh, so that was *you*." Detective Marlowe pulled a notepad from her jeans and jotted down a few lines. Then she suddenly stood up. "Well, I guess that's everything, then." She held her hand out, and I shook it, painfully aware that *my* hand was cold and clammy. "Thank you for speaking with me, Noah."

I started to relax a bit as we walked to the front door.

"Officer James," she called into the kitchen. "I'll be out front." The policeman talking to my parents nodded, then went back to taking notes. From where I stood, I could see both Mom and Dad. They looked pale, as if it were a shock to have police officers in the house.

Detective Marlowe's hand closed on the doorknob. "Oh, there is *one* other thing, Noah," she said, pausing. "Something that doesn't quite dovetail. You never asked me about why I came to talk to your parents in the first place. Why is that?"

It's a trap!

"I guess I'm a little punchy," I said, laughing nervously. "Because I'm up so late and everything. Why did you come here?" Now I concentrated on not looking guilty. *You're going to be fine,* I assured myself, thinking of the green hoodie. *You already hid the evidence.*

Detective Marlowe turned the doorknob, but kept her eyes on me. "One of your neighbors reported something unusual."

As the door opened, I heard a deep rumble from outside. Behind Detective Marlowe, I spotted a giant flatbed truck backing slowly down the street. The massive truck eased into our small driveway.

"We're ready to bring the crane!" someone shouted.

Detective Marlowe gave me a keen look. "Come with me, Noah," she said, walking out and turning briskly to the right. She popped the latch to the side gate, and waved me ahead into the narrow side yard.

In front of me, I could see that our backyard was bathed in harsh artificial light—it was lit up like an outdoor stadium.

Confused, I stopped.

"Keep going," Detective Marlowe said.

I kept going. After a few more steps, I was at the corner of the house and could see our whole backyard. Bright lights running off extension cords were perched all along the fence, lighting up a scene that looked like a Hollywood set.

There, stacked between my parents' playground models, were giant piles of lumber. There were beams and boards and posts and trusses. There were heaps of planks and braces twice my height. There was enough wood in our backyard to build a whole neighborhood. And parked in the back corners of the yard, like two huge bookends—

"One of your neighbors spotted the bulldozers." Detective Marlowe had come up on my right. "They were the ones who called the police."

I looked just beyond the policewoman, at the back of our house. Starting at the corner, thick posts stood neatly propped up against it all the way to the screen door at the far side. And leaning against the posts were short survey stakes with bright-red ribbons. Hundreds of them.

I guess EXPROPRIATE *doesn't mean "subtract" after all,* I thought.

Feeling dizzy, I reached out a hand to the closest post for support. But as soon as I touched it, the post slid away and hit the one next to it. That one quickly hit the next post, and there was a noisy chain reaction of toppling posts collapsing sideways into a big heap.

The police officer and I stared at the mess.

"Oops," I said.

"How strange," said Detective Marlowe. "Those posts were balanced there quite carefully. But why? I can't think of a reasonable explanation for *any* of this. But that's a nice crowning touch, don't you think?"

She pointed at the Möbius Fun Climb playground model, the one I'd fallen off so many times. There, perched on top of it, was a big sign. On it, parents waved to their kids as they threw a football. The sign proclaimed:

WELCOME TO THE FUTURE HOME OF CATARACT GROVE

29

I couldn't sleep.

Sure, the work crew was moving giant piles of lumber right outside my window. But even without the noise and bright lights, my mind was fluttering.

See, I'd been trying to use my "five-finger" method on the quincunx to contact T'wirpo, but so far, no dice. I glanced at my clock: 2:17 A.M.? *Great.*

I climbed out of bed and went in the kitchen to pour myself a glass of rice milk. Then I stepped out the back door and watched two forklifts lifting piles of lumber. Workmen swarmed everywhere. The closest one to me was a big bearded guy wearing a hard hat. He gave me a friendly smile as he lifted the last of the posts that I'd knocked over.

"Hey, sorry about the noise." He pointed a gloved hand at the bulldozers. "We'll have to take out part of your neighbor's fence to get those 'dozers out." The man scratched his hard hat like he was scratching his head. "But how do you think they got *in*?"

I quoted Detective Marlowe: "I have no reasonable explanation."

The man chuckled. "I'll have to remember that when I get home. 'Where have you been all night, dear?' 'I have no reasonable explanation.'" He went back to pulling a heavy strap around a big stack of boards.

"So where's all this stuff gonna go?" I asked.

"Oh, right back where it came from," the bearded man grunted, tightening the strap. "It's a rush job, which is why we're working all night. That way, they should be able to start construction just a day or so behind schedule."

"*What?*"

Seeing my crestfallen expression, the man said, "Hey, cheer up, kid. Nothing was actually lost. And building houses out at Cataract Grove gives people jobs."

"Yeah, but how long do those jobs last?" I asked. "A few weeks? And then they're gone. But Noyd Woods has been there for hundreds—*thousands*—of years!"

The worker held up his hands in surrender. "Look, kid, everyone's got an opinion. So if you think squirrels and pinecones are more important than people, that's okay with me. But me, I'm sticking up for my own species."

I didn't have anything to say to that, so I took another sip of rice milk.

* * *

The bulldozers were fired up with twin diesel roars. As they lumbered through the hole in the fence, a crane lifted lumber out of the backyard and into our driveway.

I peeked around the side of the house and saw TV crews were filming out front. I even saw Rayla Rafferty (*"I'm here LIVE!"*) talking to our neighbors, Mr. and Mrs. Shuey. Luckily, the police had rolled out yellow crime scene tape across our front yard, so we were safe inside the house.

I got back into bed, feeling hopeless, my mind racing. *How did I mix Mom and Dad up in this? Are they going to be charged with Grand Theft Bulldozer?* I was so full of adrenaline from everything that had happened, there was no way I was ever going to—

I fell into a deep sleep.

At sunrise, Mom and Dad woke me. They both had bags under their eyes, and I felt like I did, too. I managed to get dressed and drag myself to the kitchen. While Dad made me an egg-white scramble, Mom explained that the two of them needed to drive down to the police station to "clear up a few more details."

"But you didn't have anything to do with this!" I protested.

Mom nodded. "The police can't prove we stole anything—because we didn't. But all those construction supplies *were* found in our backyard." She paused and looked at Dad. "It's all very strange."

My conscience twinged. "But shouldn't I come with you?"

My parents smiled at me—never suspecting that *I* was the real criminal.

"That's thoughtful, Noah," said Dad. "But you didn't have anything to do with this. As for your mother and me, we have a little history with the police, and that doesn't help. In fact, you could almost say we're jailbirds."

"Never mind that," said Mom, giving Dad a warning glance. "Anyway, we've asked Mr. Bright if you can hang out with the twins this morning."

And so, an hour later the three of us were dressed, ready to go, and standing at the front door. Of course, I had the quincunx with me. And then it was time for what Dad called "running the gauntlet."

"Ready?" asked Mom.

Dad and I nodded.

Mom swung the door open and waved us forward. "Go, go, go!"

Instantly, cameras swung our way. Packs of reporters on the sidewalk broke up as they ran for microphones and started sprinting toward us.

"This is Rayla Rafferty LIVE from the suspects' home—"
"What can you tell us about the playgrounds you built in Russia, Mr. Grow—"
"Noah, what do you know about—"

After a quick blur of motion, three car doors slammed shut a moment later.

"*Whew,*" said Mom, turning the key and driving quickly past the parked news vans. "If this is what reporters do to innocent people, I feel sorry for the guilty ones."

"Me too," I said, feeling sorry for myself.

A few moments later, I got out of the station wagon and stood by the gleaming new fire hydrant in front of the Brights' house. Dad rolled down his window, and Mom leaned forward from the driver's seat. "Remember honey, we're *not* under arrest. The police are as confused as we are."

Dad gave me a thumbs-up. "For now, let's think of this as an interesting mystery. It's like that thing J. R. R. Tolkien said."

Mom smiled. "He said a lot of things, honey."

"Wait, I've got it." Dad leaned forward. "*An adventure is just a hardship looked at the right way.* So what we're having is an adventure. Don't worry, Noah, and we'll see you soon."

I didn't want to ruin their positive attitude. So as the car pulled away, I waved and cheerily called out, "Have fun at the police station!"

I watched them drive off, passing a boy by the side of the road. He was sitting on his bike—his orange bike—and holding something in his hands.

There's that kid again! I started to walk toward him, half-expecting him to pedal off. As I approached, the boy slipped whatever he'd been holding into the side pocket of his backpack. Then he let his arms hang down at his sides, like a robot whose power had been switched off.

"Hey," I said.

"Hi! Do you remember me?" He spoke fast, in a surprisingly deep, raspy voice. "I was in the bathroom that day with Coby."

"Yeah, I remember—sorry about that. So what's up? What're you doing here?"

His words tumbled out quickly. "I'm Sanjay. And I'm here looking for you."

SANJAY *(Dux survivors)*

APPEARANCE: A roundish boy with an intense gaze, and hair like an artichoke that's gone to seed. Looks startled and excited at the same time.

VOICE: Deep and hoarse, like a substitute teacher who's been yelling.

PLUMAGE: Dressed like a cartoon character. Currently wearing skater sneakers, bright-green shorts, and an orange T-shirt that says LET THE KIDS IN FOR FREE.

RANGE: Unknown.

SOCIAL BEHAVIOR: Almost always seen with three other kids his age.

STATUS: Additional observation needed.

"Um, how *old* are you?" I asked.

Sanjay looked around warily. "Me? I'm nine and five-sixths years," he said. "But that's not important right now. There's something you have to know—"

"NOAH!" called Jason from behind me. "Let's go—we've got stuff to do!"

Sanjay raised his robot arms up to the handlebars. "Okay, you really need to talk to me and my friends." Sanjay glanced at his wristwatch. "Seven hours from . . . *now* . . . it will be three o'clock. Meet us up by the waterfall then, okay?"

He turned his bike around before I could say anything, and looked back at me over his shoulder. "More later."

I stood there, speechless, as Sanjay pedaled off.

Interesting kid, I thought, walking back to the Brights' house. *Who says "More later"?*

But the day had other surprises waiting for me. Because when Jason and Jenny met me at their front door, they were still in their pajamas—their matching Star Wars pajamas.

"I thought you said you weren't going to do anything crazy?" Jason whisper-hissed. "But then you took those bulldozers! And who was that little kid, anyway?"

"That's no kid," I said. "That's Sanjay. He's nine and five-sixths years old."

"Whatever. Did you know that you're all over the news?" Jenny demanded, looking up from her cell phone. "And everyone from school is freaking out about this thing."

Mr. Bright interrupted from the kitchen. "IGNORE THEM, NOAH. NOW, WHO WANTS WAFFLES?"

Of course, we all did. (Sure, I'd already *had* breakfast, but probiotic egg-white scrambles never stick with me.)

"Let's duck into my office," said Jason. "We can eat there."

A moment later, I was throwing T-shirts off the chair by Jason's desk. Jenny bulldozed her way in over dirty socks and empty boxes of Cheez-Its. "Okay, Noah," she said. "So how'd you get caught red-handed with a whole housing development in your backyard?"

"Actually," I said, "my *parents* were caught red-handed. And that's the problem." I launched into the story, leaving out one small detail—my chat with T'wirpo, the alien from an unknown POO.

Why didn't I tell the twins? Partly, it was because I didn't think they'd believe me. I mean, I could imagine the conversation:

"You guys, I need to let you in on something about the quincunx."

"Yes?"

"I mean, I don't think there's any harm in letting you know."

"Go ahead."

"I guess the key thing is for you to keep open minds about what I'm about to share."

"Got it. Fire away."

"Well, you might be surprised to know that the quincunx was grown on a faraway planet. And then it was sent here by an alien!"

[*long pause*]

"Dude, shut up."

Or maybe the truth is that I just didn't want to share Zorcha T'wirpo with them. Like, knowing an alien was *my* secret. (Yeah, yeah, selfish, I know.)

Anyway, a few minutes later, I wrapped up: "—and then I used EXPROPRIATE on pretty much everything." Sighing, I crossed my arms across my chest. "Looks like I messed up, big-time."

"Don't feel bad," said Jenny. "It could have happened to anyone."

"Thanks."

Jason snorted. "Yeah, anyone who screwed up in the exact same way Noah did. Look, you said the bulldozers disappeared, just like everything else. But you should have known there was no way that stuff could just *vanish*." He gave Jenny a meaningful look.

"You mean everything has to go *somewhere*, right?" said Jenny. "I get it."

I didn't get it.

"C'mon, Noah," implored Jason. "We did 'conservation of mass' in, like, the first month of science class."

"Oh!" Jason was talking about a lab experiment. We weighed tiny amounts of two different chemicals. Then we combined the chemicals in a big empty beaker. And BAM—the beaker filled all the way with green foam. *Lots* of green foam.

Finally, we weighed the overflowing beaker. And it was the exact *same* weight as the total of our two earlier measurements.

In other words, nothing was added or lost. So—

"'Mass cannot be created or destroyed,'" I recited. "That means the wood and bulldozers couldn't just *disappear*. But what a rip-off—I didn't know all that stuff was going to MY house!"

"And speaking of rip-offs," Jenny pointed out, "that means you stole all that stuff the police found."

"But I didn't mean to *steal* it," I protested. "I meant to *destroy* it."

"So you just committed the wrong crime?" Jenny laughed sarcastically. "I guess that makes it okay."

I shrugged. "Well, I didn't know what 'expropriate' meant."

Jenny pecked at her cell phone. "'*Expropriate*: to take property away from its owner.'"

"So I didn't actually steal." That made me feel a little better. "I just expropriated!"

Still reading, Jenny added, "Synonym: to steal."

I stopped feeling better, but Jason perked right up. "So you can just move things from one spot to your backyard? Wow, let's think about this. What if we took a trip to the sports store today and you—"

Mr. Bright came into the room, balancing three plates of waffles on his arms. Sidestepping a comic book, he sniffed the air suspiciously. "JASON, WHAT'S THAT SMELL?"

I took a whiff. Besides the usual odors of dirty laundry and body spray, I didn't smell anything.

After handing each of us a plate, Mr. Bright's nose led him to Jason's closet. He bent over, and like a dog digging a hole, started flinging shoes, empty sports-drink bottles, and comic books behind him. "JASON! WHAT IS *THIS*?" He held up what looked like a small, moldy pie.

Jason was mildly surprised. "A calzone."

"A *WHAT*?"

"A calzone," Jason explained. "It's like a pizza sandwich, with meat and cheese in the middle—"

"I KNOW WHAT A CALZONE IS!" cried Mr. Bright. "BUT *WHY* IS A CALZONE IN YOUR CLOSET?"

Jason looked genuinely puzzled. "That's a good question, actually."

The phone started to ring in the other room. Mr. Bright just snorted and left, taking the moldy calzone with him.

I took a forkful of waffle. It had blueberries in it and was drenched in maple syrup. "Your dad is so cool," I said. After chewing and swallowing, I yawned so hard, my jaw cracked. I was *really* tired. All I wanted to do was eat some waffles and not think about anything important.

But Jenny wasn't letting me off that easily. She pointed her fork at me. "So right now, the police think your mom and dad are thieves?"

"It's just totally lame," I complained. "My parents are obviously innocent. And how was I supposed to know that something *I* did would reflect badly on *them*?"

Jason and Jenny both paused, forkfuls of waffle halfway to their mouths. Then the twins started laughing hysterically.

"What?" I asked.

Mr. Bright knocked briefly and came in. "I'M JUST PLANNING AHEAD FOR LATER TODAY. SO HOW DOES PIZZA SOUND FOR LUNCH, NOAH?"

"Thanks, Mr. Bright," I said, "but my parents should be back pretty soon."

Mr. Bright shifted uncomfortably. "ACTUALLY, I JUST GOT A CALL FROM THE STATION. IT SOUNDS LIKE YOUR MOM AND DAD ARE GOING TO BE THERE A WHILE. SO IS DEEP-DISH PEPPERONI OKAY?"

30

A LONG TIME AGO—LAST WEEK, TO BE EXACT—I WAS young and innocent.

But I've grown up a lot since then. Now I know that the world is totally unfair. Just look at what's happened in the last few days:

—A bunch of little kids were nearly electrocuted.
—My dad's peanut butter got a new flavor: *fire.*
—An earthquake almost destroyed my school.
—My parents were behind bars for a crime they had nothing to do with.
—The black swifts were likely gone forever.

"What good have I done?" I asked out loud. But the words were lost in the quiet roar of the waterfall. You know how criminals always return to the scene of the crime? That was me. From my seat on a flat rock, the big ferns waved in the breeze. Beyond them, the surveying stakes had been replanted everywhere. And soon, bulldozer tracks would crush the ferns and uproot the trees.

I glared at the sparkling device in my hand. "And what good are *you*?"

Stupid quincunx. I felt like my sparkling discovery was actually just part of a long, practical joke on me. I was tired of it!

Plik-plik-plik-plik.

I whipped my head around. *The black swifts are still here? How is that possible?* Black swifts are famous for being super-cautious around humans. *Why would they stay?*

The baby swift called to its parents.

Plik-plik-plik-plik?

Of course. The black swifts couldn't move somewhere with a hatchling in the nest. But once the bulldozers started ripping up the earth by their hidden home, what choice would they have?

Black swifts nested in the most remote places possible. They went out of their way to be out of the way. But just like the passenger pigeons, these swifts *still* somehow ended up in front of the swerving SUV called Cataract Grove.

I'd tried to help the little birds. I had the quincunx, and even took advice from an alien to make sure my plan worked. But when I tried to do something good, my plan backfired on me. And when I did something *bad,* my plan backfired on my parents!

I wanted to curse, to yell, to break something. For the umpteenth time, I used my five fingertips on the back of the quincunx to try to contact T'wirpo. For the umpteenth time, I got nothing.

That does it. Standing, I cocked my arm back to throw the quincunx into the pool—

And then sweet music rang out. *"Greet-ings! You have a mess-age! Oh, greet-ings! You please check your mess-age!"*

The quincunx's screen was blinking red. I tapped it feverishly. I was all set to complain to T'wirpo, to protest, to demand.

GREETINGS, NOAH, the words flashed. THE QUINCUNX HAS ASKED ME TO RELAY THAT IT WOULD PREFER NOT TO GO UNDER-WATER. IT FINDS ALGAE DISTASTEFUL.

"Don't worry, I won't," I said reassuringly, as much to the quincunx as the unseen alien. "But, T'wirpo, I need some answers. Like, you *grew* the quincunx, but it can make its own decisions? And why do I have it at all?"

APOLOGIES! FOR NOW I FEAR THAT YOU MUST EMBRACE SOME OF THESE MYSTERIES. The quincunx scrolled up on T'wirpo's message at the exact rate I was reading. BUT I CAN SHARE THAT YOUR USE OF THE QUINCUNX IS FOR A CLASS PROJ-ECT ON HUMANS. I CHOSE YOU AS AN OUTSTANDING SPECI-MEN OF YOUR SPECIES.

I puffed up proudly. *Hey, I'm an outstanding specimen!* I

thought of an animal researcher tagging a bird with a tracking chip or band to study its species' migrations and other behaviors. And right now, I was that bird! *Maybe this is for T'wirpo's science fair project! It could be called "The Human Equation: How to Help the People of Earth."*

NOAH, MY PARENTAL UNITS AGREE THAT IT IS ONLY RIGHT FOR ME TO MAKE SOME CONTACTS WITH YOU. I HAVE 42 PARENTAL UNITS. THEY SERVE SIMILAR FUNCTIONS TO YOUR "MOM" AND "DAD."

"Wait a minute," I said. "How old are you?"

YOU CALCULATE HUMAN AGE BY PLANETARY ROTATIONS AROUND YOUR STAR, YES? SO YOU ARE 11 AND I AM 727 YEARS OLD.

"But that means you're *ancient*," I cried. "Aren't you a little old for your parents to be telling you what to do?"

MY PLANET ROTATES MUCH MORE QUICKLY AROUND OUR STAR THAN YOURS. IN EARTH YEARS, I AM YOUNGER THAN THIS FIGURE.

"Okay." I thought about that. "So how old are you in Earth years?"

SEVEN.

"Seven?!" I was talking with an alien first grader.

MY PARENTAL UNITS SAY I AM VERY MATURE FOR MY AGE.

"Well, *my* parental units are in jail right now."

YES. IN MY INEXPERIENCE WITH YOUR PLANET, I SOMETIMES MAKE MISTAKES.

"Yeah. And one of those mistakes is this quincunx's menu. I can't understand what most of its words mean!"

If it's possible for a text message to look surprised, this one was.

BUT THE QUINCUNX KNOWS ALL 1,025,120 OF YOUR ENGLISH LANGUAGE WORDS.

"Yeah, but *I* don't!" I protested.

OH.

There was a pause as Zorcha T'wirpo tried to understand why I didn't know my own language.

IT SEEMS I DID NOT TAKE INTO CONSIDERATION HUMAN BRAIN SIZE. Then the quincunx flashed a new message—

PLEASE CHECK THE ADEPTNESS MENU.

—before blinking back to the green home screen.

"Hello?" I stared at the quincunx. Nothing. "He hung up on me. Or *she* hung up on me."

I looked up at the sky. Somewhere, way out there, was an alien kid on an unknown POO.

"*It* hung up on me?"

31

I opened the quincunx's Adeptness menu, and there were only two choices—**?** or **!**.

Great—simple is good, but now I'm just getting punctuation marks?

T'wirpo may have been trying to make things easier for me. But by going *so* simple, the alien had kept things just as mysterious as before!

Even so, of the two possibilities, the exclamation mark seemed more clear-cut. If I used it, *something* dramatic would happen. But what? The question mark's meaning was more up in the air. Was it a warning? A prank? Or what?

I glared at the quincunx. "I hope you're having fun."

It just gleamed innocently. It was like the quincunx was saying, *There is* always *a choice, human.*

Then the baby black swift called:

Plik-plik-plik-plik.

"But I don't really have any choice, do I?" I asked. Because I had to do *something* for the black swifts—even if I didn't know what that something was.

I made my decision. Both the quincunx and T'wirpo knew I had questions—so maybe this was their way of offering to answer them. I made my choice and watched the screen flash:

?

?

?

I felt the connection being made.

Yikes!

Energy surged into my body. It clenched my fists and curled my toes. I felt light-headed and carefree—and *fizzy*, like I'd just chugged a soda.

Suddenly, I needed air, so I gulped in a lungful. Ah, that was good. But I needed MORE air. Another deep breath. I felt so giddy, I laughed and—

"Hello?" called a woman's voice from behind me.

I spun around in surprise. Two people were at the head of the Nature Trail. One was a well-dressed woman with gray streaks in her hair and a smile on her lips. Next to her was a man in a green-and-brown suit. He had a neatly trimmed mustache, and he was holding a computer tablet.

"I beg your pardon," the woman said. "Please don't let us

interrupt you." The pair began talking quietly and looking at the survey stakes. While they did, Mustache Man took notes.

My hand clenched around the quincunx as anger rose inside me. They obviously worked for Cataract Grove. Maybe these two even owned the company—and here they were, planning this waterfall's destruction.

That meant they were the enemy of the black swifts. And any enemy of the black swifts was *my* enemy, too. Of course, they hadn't counted on me being here to stop them.

I closed my eyes and tried to get a feel for whatever the quincunx had set loose inside me. But it was slippery. Catching **?** was like trying to grab the string of a runaway balloon. Gulping more air, I chased **?**, grabbed for it and missed, reached for it again—

And then I caught the string! Immediately, something odd happened with my feet. I opened my eyes and noticed that the ferns at my feet were farther away. *What are they doing down there? Did the world just shrink?*

In the background, I could hear Mustache Man murmuring: "—I think the environmental damage here has been minimal—"

And then I realized what had happened. *The world didn't shrink—I just grew taller.* But that wasn't right either. I looked down at my feet. I was still the same height as before, but I was . . . floating.

I'm lifting off—I'M FLYING!

32

I SOARED IN THE AIR, THE WIND BLOWING ACROSS my face. *I'm as free as a bird!* It was hard to fully enjoy the moment, though, because I was mostly trying not to pee my pants.

Seriously—I was TERRIFIED. And I know that might seem sort of weird. After all, I love birds, and most birds fly. Some even spend days in the air, drifting along with the wind, perfectly safe. I mean, scientists tracked one little shorebird, a bar-tailed godwit (*Limosa lapponica*), from Alaska to New Zealand. That's over seven thousand miles—and it never landed once!

So it's not like I'm afraid of heights. . . . Okay, I actually *am* afraid of heights. But just in the normal way that most people are. You know, like how when you get on the high dive at the pool, and it's obvious that you're so far up that when you jump you're going to miss the pool completely and smash into the concrete?

Yeah. *That* way.

So after the quincunx launched me into the heavens, I squeezed my eyes shut. And I kept them shut as the air whistled past my ears and clawed at my hair. Far, far away, I could still hear the voices of Mustache Man and the Gray Streak Woman.

Was I a hundred feet above Noyd Falls? *Two* hundred? There was only one way to find out. I brought a shaking hand up to my face and fearfully peeked through my fingers—

I was in the exact same spot as before. Except now I was hovering about eight inches over the rock.

So I AM flying—but I guess my imagination got the best of me.

The call of a black swift swept the little canyon.

Plik-plik-plik-plik.

The woman gasped. "Is that—"

"Look!" said Mustache Man, pointing to the waterfall. "That's the positive identification we need!"

A bird crawled out from behind the rushing waters of Noyd Falls. The swift's long black wings were crossed behind its back like swords. It cocked its head to the side and shot us a sharp glance.

The woman almost clapped her hands in glee. "So the bird is still here!"

Wait a minute, I thought. *What's going on?*

"Hey," I whispered from my newfound height. "Why do *you* care about that bird?"

Without even glancing my way, Mustache Man said, "That's not just *any* bird, young man," he said. "It's a—"

"—black swift," I finished.

That got their attention. As the two of them turned to me, I got a sinking feeling (without actually sinking). I'd drawn attention to the fact that I was flying!

The man and woman looked at me with interest—but neither one freaked out. *Why not?* Then I realized that giant ferns were surrounding my legs. So from their view, it just looked like I was perched on an unseen rock or log.

The black swift leaped from the mossy cliff, flew in a tight circle, then shot beyond our view, leaving the three of us craning our necks to follow its flight.

"Excuse me," the woman said to me, "but did you happen to file a Rare Wildlife Sighting report a few days ago?"

"How'd you know that?" I asked.

"So you're *Noah Grow*?" Mustache Man said my name like he was as amazed as me. And *that* was when I saw the round, yellow seal on the front of Mustache Man's jacket. It had a flying duck on it—the symbol of the U.S. Department of Fish and Wildlife.

I nodded.

"Pleased to meet you! My name is Garr Dion. I processed your form."

"And after that, Mr. Dion contacted *me*," said the woman. "I'm Noelle Noyd." She came forward, holding out her hand.

Uh-oh—can't let her see my legs!

I tried to step toward Noelle Noyd, but it felt like I was inside a bouncy, inflatable castle. Somehow I bobbed forward a little, and the ferns pressed up against my legs and covered my floating feet.

Although Noelle Noyd's eyes widened at my bumbling, she politely kept walking toward me. So I reached out and took her hand as she said, "It's a pleasure to meet you—*oh!*"

As soon as I touched her, *Noelle Noyd* seemed to rise in the air! I let go of her fingers—and she dipped back down, lost her balance, and fell into a pile of ferns.

"Sorry!" I said. "Are you alright?" Noelle Noyd got to her feet and gave me the kind of look you'd give to a kid whose hobby is floating in ferns. And then the importance of the woman's name sank in. "Wait, are you one of the *Noyd Woods* Noyds?"

"I am," said Noelle Noyd, dusting the fern spores off her pants. "It's a pleasure to meet you, Noah. In fact, it's even been . . . *uplifting*," she added, slyly.

As for Garr Dion, he was grinning so hard, it looked painful. "Young man, it's a *real* pleasure to meet you!"

"And for me." Noelle Noyd gestured around us. "Noah, these woods have belonged to my family for three generations. After my parents passed away, my brothers—Norris and Nathan—and I inherited it. I've always loved it here, so I was stunned when my brothers wanted sell off Noyd Woods. Of course, I argued against the sale, but in the end, I was outvoted."

She pointed to the survey stakes. "When I found that Norris and Nathan had hired a construction company to begin work, I was heartbroken. And then, just as this"—she made a disgusted face—"this *Cataract Grove* development got under way, I got word from Mr. Dion about the black swift.

"Mr. Dion went to my brothers to argue the case against developing this land. And the beautiful thing is that they actually listened. Between this unique species and the community pressure to leave Noyd Woods open to the public, my brothers actually changed their minds!"

I wasn't sure I understood. "So Cataract Grove is postponed?"

"No." Noelle Noyd smiled. "Cataract Grove is *cancelled*."

A wave of joy and relief swept over me. *Yes! Wow! Epic! Wait, does anyone say "epic" anymore? I don't care!* I really wanted to dish out a high five, but didn't want to make anyone float.

Instead, I bobbed slightly up and down.

As a rugged outdoors guy, Garr Dion didn't let that scare him. (Or he just didn't notice.) "Noah, you must already know that there may be only a few dozen black swift colonies in the United States," he said, "so habitat conservation like this is key for the species to survive."

Plik-plik-plik-plik.

Mr. Dion blinked as another black swift emerged from

behind the falls. Upon seeing us, it stopped.

"So now we know there are two adults!" Dion said. "The first black swift must be foraging for food while this one keeps an eye on the chick."

And right on cue, the baby swift cheeped from behind the waterfall.

Plik-plik-plik-plik.

"We're very lucky," said Noelle Noyd. "And I think Noah here is the reason why." Then she snapped her fingers. "Wait, you said your last name is *Grow*? Isn't it your backyard where the police found the bulldozers?"

"Yeah, but I don't know how they got there," I said, adding, "there's no reasonable explanation." *Just like there's no explanation for why the quincunx is making me float in the air right now.*

"How mysterious!" Noelle Noyd pressed her lips together and looked thoughtful. "There seems to be more to you than meets the eye, Noah. But rest easy. I'll see to it that my family doesn't press charges. If anything, we owe *you* a favor."

My parents aren't going to jail! My parents aren't going to jail! I was so happy, I didn't know what to say.

So I just kept hovering in the air.

Noelle Noyd turned her head from me to scan the sky, and Mr. Dion started taking notes on his tablet. And that gave me a chance to press the quincunx's stem.

And then, to my surprise, I gave a mighty "BUUURRRRP!"

It sounded like the belch of a water buffalo, or Jason after he chugged a soda.

"Wow, excuse me," I said, as my epic flight ended with a gentle drop back to the ground—and my normal height.

I felt short.

As I slipped the quincunx into my pocket, Noelle Noyd turned to watch me curiously. "Noah, I'd love to talk to you," she said. "You look like a great weight's been lifted from your shoulders."

"What can I say?" I said, beaming like a goofball. "I like birds!"

33

In a happy daze, I said good-bye to Noelle Noyd and Garr Dion. Then I bounced down the Nature Trail.

Things were looking up!

But then I reached the trailhead by the road and saw *two* automobiles parked by the Cataract Grove sign. One was an empty sedan with a "U.S. Fish and Wildlife Service" emblem on the door. The other was a pickup truck with green camouflage flames painted on the front.

Uh-oh.

Two heads in the truck's cab turned toward me.

"That's him!" said Coby Cage from the passenger seat. The driver's door opened, and Brock got out. He started running toward me, his heavy combat boots crunching on the dry soil.

BROCK CAGE *(Impalus excubitor)*

APPEARANCE: See entry for "Coby Cage"—now increase size and buffness.

PLUMAGE: Short-cropped hair. Multiple tattoos of fire, skulls, and barbed wire. Currently wearing tight black T-shirt with the words SEARCH AND DESTROY.

RANGE: He has a truck.

SOCIAL BEHAVIOR: Rumored to be expert in Mixed Martial Arts. This would mean this specimen fights other large, tough life-forms and then beats on them like drums.

STATUS: Does not appear to be kid-friendly.

What to do? There was no time to use the quincunx, and I was too weak in the knees to run.

Suddenly I thought of the Arabian babbler (*Turdoides squamiceps*). It's not a very tough bird, but if a cat or an owl attacks it, the babbler won't fly off. Instead, the bird bluffs. It will actually attack its predator *first*, while making a loud call that sounds like *"tzwick!"*

This call signals all the other Arabian babblers to answer

the alarm—and the next thing you know, a feathery mob of babblers gathers to drive off the predator.

Of course, I didn't have a gang to call for help. And yelling "*tzwick!*" probably wasn't going to be much use, either. But like I told you, I've had practice bluffing. And now it was time for me to harness the mysterious powers of Fake-Fu.

So as Brock ran up, I started dancing my hands around in front of my face. "*Waaaah!*" I warned him in a high-pitched call. Then I let loose a jabber of low, croaking vowels—followed by a fighting scream.

"*Hai-bojo-gween-socky! OOO-YAH!*"

Brock slid to a stop in front of me, paralyzed by fear.

It worked? Good one, Arabian babbler!

Then he laughed. "Kid, those are the fakest moves I've ever seen," he said in a surprisingly quiet voice. "It's like you took a Tae Kwon Do class once, but never made it to Kwon or Do."

Cracking his tattooed knuckles, Brock leaned in and dropped his voice. "Listen, I was actually hoping we wouldn't find you. But my brother won't let this go. For some reason, you remind Coby of our dad."

"Um—is that bad?" I asked.

"Very." Brock sighed, and he gave me a pained half-smile. "Dad bailed on us when Coby was eight. And we haven't seen him since. All that he left behind were unpaid bills and bird books."

"Wait—your dad was a *birder*?"

"Yeah. Birds were one of the only things he really cared about." Brock glanced back at his brother with a fond look, maybe even tender. "Ever since, Coby has thrown himself into computers. He refuses to even talk about Dad. And as for you, Coby also insists you did *something* to him."

"Hurry up, Brock!" yelled Coby from the truck. "Get him before he does something weird!"

Brock sighed. "So now I have to 'do something.' Trust me, it's better that I do this than Coby. Just so you know what to expect, I'll start with a simple leg sweep. Go with it and try to land gently. Then I'll lightly punch your face. Remember, I'm a pro. You'll barely feel it."

Yay. I'm going to have my face punched lightly.

And with that, Brock raised his hambone fists and came forward. "Relax, kid," he said soothingly. "You're going to be just fine."

Oh, well. I closed my eyes and steeled myself. After all, Brock knew how to hit opponents who were expert in kung fu, jiujitsu, judo, kickboxing, and karate. But did he know how to hit a birder? I was about to find out.

With my eyes shut, I sensed that there was a remnant of **?** still inside me. *If my Arabian babbler defense hadn't helped me, could the quincunx?*

Desperately I grabbed at **?**'s runaway balloon string—and I caught it.

With a loud gasp, I gulped in a double-lungful of air, and

my sneakers lifted off from the dirt. And as I opened my eyes, Brock stepped forward and gracefully dropped to the ground, swinging his leg out beneath me.

But his leg sweep only met thin air—because I was floating again!

Brock popped back up to his feet incredibly fast—where he found me bobbing at his eye level. I could almost read his thoughts: *This kid must have jumped in the air . . . but why is he staying* up?

Brock didn't seem scared of the floating boy with giant ears in front of him. Instead, he looked curious. "That's remarkable," he said. "Do you know you're floating?"

"Yeah, I know," I said.

Meanwhile, Coby saw what was happening. He slid to the driver's seat and honked the truck's horn. "Brock, get out of there before he makes your guts show!"

Brock hesitated. "That seems unlikely, Coby," he called back.

"Hurry!" Coby started the truck up and revved the engine.

I don't know if Brock was more worried about the floating kid in front of him or Coby driving his truck. But either way, he turned and ran, his boots spitting up gravel behind him. Then, to my shock, he opened the truck's door, pulled Coby from the cab, and started to drag him over to where I was floating.

Or where I *was* floating. Because as Brock grabbed Coby, the last traces of ? vanished, and with a quiet little burp, I dropped to the ground. It was a short drop, but I still managed to land on my butt.

"Unusual situations require creative solutions," Brock said as I picked myself up. "So let's get everything out in the open. Coby, what's your issue with Noah?"

Coby pulled himself free from his brother's grip and sullenly avoided looking at me. "I don't talk about Noah. He's dead to me."

"Whoa!" Brock held up his hands in alarm. "That's a little harsh, don't you think?"

Coby reluctantly sighed. "Okay, Noah's just *nearly* dead to me. He's like, gasping for breath and barely hanging on to life by a thin thread."

"See, *now* we're making progress!" Brock said encouragingly. "Now then, what exactly do you have against this guy?"

"*He* knows what he did."

I couldn't believe my ears. "What *I* did? I can't help it that I'm a birder. And it's your own fault that your skin turned invisible!"

"That's not what I mean," said Coby. "Think back to the first time you saw me."

I thought back. "You stole my glasses."

"Nope, that was the *second* time you saw me. I'm talking about the very first day of classes, when we were in fourth grade."

What was Coby talking about? On my first day at Robert

F. Moral School, my parents had dropped me off (for once!). I went to my classes. At the end of the day, I took the bus home— And then I realized what Coby was getting at.[7]

"Oh, yeah!" I looked at Coby questioningly. "Do you mean the thing with the bus seat? That was you?"

Brock laughed. "Hey, you must be the kid who offered to *share* the seat! Even I heard about *that*." He looked at me with something like appreciation. "You're just full of surprises."

Coby grimly nodded. "Some surprise. That was *my* bus on *my* route. And everyone heard about the kid who got away with stealing *my* seat."

"Seriously. A bus seat?" *THIS was why Coby hates me? I upset the pecking order on the bus?* "I did offer to scooch over, you know."

Coby pursed his lips. "True," he admitted. He glanced at his brother and sighed. "Dude, I guess I overreacted. Mr. Gillespie's working with me on not doing that so much."

Brock clapped his hands. "So we're good here? Nice work,

---

7. **FIELD NOTES: Grade Four, Day One**

After climbing aboard the bus, I found it nearly full.

"Try the back," suggested the bearded driver, Mr. Berry.

I worked my way down the aisle and finally found one entire seat at the back that was empty. So I sat in it and looked out the window.

A few moments later, a voice said, "That's my seat."

With nowhere else to go, I grabbed my backpack and I slid over in the seat, saying, "Let's share."

Then I looked up to find Mr. Berry steering some tall kid up to a spot near the front of the bus. And I didn't give it another thought.

gentlemen. Now shake hands—good. Coby, let's get home. I'll even let you drive part of the way."

Coby's eyes lit up. "Really?"

A moment later, the two of them got in the cab. Coby rolled down the driver's side window and called over to me. "Hey, Noah," he said. "You know how Anemona tricked you into handing over your thingamajig?"

"Yeah?"

Coby revved the engine. "Just so you know, that was *all* her idea." And with that, he shoved the truck into gear. "See ya."

He hit the gas and the truck lurched backward, snapping off one of the posts for the big Cataract Grove sign. As Coby locked up the brakes, the sign teetered and half-fell into the truck's bed.

"Stop!" Brock yelled.

Coby stopped.

"Now scoot over."

Coby scooted.

Brock walked around the back of the truck to look at the damage. The truck seemed fine, but the sign had twisted around into the truck's bed, and even repeated tugs wouldn't free it. "I'm going to have to pull forward," he said. Brock got in the cab and gave me a mock salute. "Hang in there, kid."

As Brock hit the gas, the big sign snapped off from its other post and fell the rest of the way into the truck with a thud. A moment later, the pickup fishtailed down the road, the Cataract Grove sign disappearing into the distance.

Watching the Cage brothers drive off, I realized something. I may have just saved the black swifts, but the quincunx had just saved me from being lightly punched in the face.

But I was still left with one burning question:

Camo flames . . . WHY?

34

THE GARAGE DOOR WAS OPEN, AND THE AIR HOCKEY game echoed down the driveway.

Pock.

"So the police released your mom and dad," said Jason, lunging for the puck. "And you saved Noyd Woods—"

Pock. Pock.

"—AND the black swifts," I added, blocking his shot.

"And you did all that," Jason continued, putting some spin on the puck, "by filling out a *form*?"

I glanced up. "Weird, huh?"

Pock. PING!

Jason raised his hands triumphantly. "And that's game!"

With a scornful snort, Jenny took my place. "I like your new hair color," I said, handing her the paddle.

"Thank you." Jenny tossed her mostly green hair back like

a model. She fished the puck out of her goal and glanced at her brother. "Ready?"

"I was *born* ready," Jason bragged, swaying from side to side like a pro, confidently spinning the paddle. In his deep-blue Golden State Warriors jersey, he actually looked like he knew what he was doing.

Jenny laughed. "Since *I* was born first, I don't think that's true." She made a sudden move.

Pock. PING!

The twins talked trash while I wondered if I should tell them the rest of the story. See, I still hadn't said anything to them about T'wirpo. I know, I know. Look, I'd *meant* to. But the longer I waited to tell them, the harder it became. And as I tried to decide how to break the news, my eyes fell on the game shelf's box of dominoes.

Dominoes.

You remember my invisible domino theory? Well, now I had a pretty good idea of who'd been setting up dominoes around me—T'wirpo.

"Hey, g-guys!"

Ronnie Ramirez came pedaling up the driveway. His bike had the biggest yellow banana seat I've ever seen. Also, the right leg of Ronnie's dress pants was stuffed in his sock. This kept his cuff from getting caught in the bike chain.

He definitely knows how to catch your attention.

"Hey, Ronnie," I said. The twins stopped playing air hockey.

They started fiddling with their paddles and avoiding eye contact. There was an awkward silence.

"Uh, why is everyone acting weird?" I asked.

Ronnie shifted uneasily on his banana seat and looked at the twins. But they were busy having a whisper argument.

"YOU tell him," hissed Jason.

"I'm not going to tell him. YOU tell him!" responded Jenny.

"Fine!" Jason turned to me with a guilty expression. "Noah, Ronnie knows everything."

I laughed, but then saw he was serious. "What does 'everything' mean, Jason?"

"You know," said Jason. "About your quincunx . . . and all that."

I'm pretty sure my eyes started to bug out of my head. "I can't believe it!" I yelled. "My own BEST FRIEND can't keep his mouth SHUT about the biggest secret—"

"Noah," Jenny interrupted, "*I'm* the one who told Ronnie."

"Oh," I took a deep breath and retracted my eyes.

Jenny came closer. "But Ronnie was smart enough to figure most of it out himself."

Hearing Jenny say something nice about him, Ronnie looked like he wanted to hug himself. But instead, he pulled his pants leg out of his sock.

"Okay, Boy Genius," I said to him, "how'd you do it?"

"R-remember on the bus with Anemona? That got me w-wondering." Ronnie kicked his kickstand down. "And then during the earthquake, you t-told me to leave school. But after *you* dis-disappeared, I saw Mrs. Sanchez, so I followed her. And I was p-peeking from the classroom door as you p-punched through that wall!"

"So you SPIED?"

"Yes, I s-spied!" Ronnie said. "And then I remembered the news story about the br-broken power pole in front of the Brights' house. The rest was ch-child's play."

I wanted to be mad, but couldn't. After all, this was *Ronnie.*

Sensing the crisis had passed, Ronnie smiled. "So am I part of the t-team?"

Jason laughed. "There isn't any 'team,' Ronnie." Then he looked at me. "Is there?"

I shrugged.

"Anyway," said Ronnie, taking off his bike helmet. "Here's an idea. I think your qu-qu-quincunx might be an advanced form of military technology. It's a w-weapon of some kind."

"Cool!" chimed in Jason. "I *knew* it."

Jenny threw the air hockey puck at him. "*You* thought it was from a reality show!"

Ronnie just ignored them. "B-b-but whether or not the quincunx IS a weapon, I don't think it was lost. That doesn't make any s-sense." He stopped, as if he had more to say but didn't want to spell it out.

Jenny was looking at Ronnie. "So you're saying . . ."

But Ronnie was looking at Jason, who was looking at Jenny.

Then I looked over at Ronnie, and now he was looking at me.

We were all looking at one another. Now we were getting somewhere!

"Ronnie," Jenny coaxed, "you're saying the quincunx's owner *knows* what Noah's been doing all along?"

Ronnie nodded enthusiastically. "Of c-course!"

"He's right." I pulled out the quincunx and seized the moment. "Actually, I got a text from its owner yesterday."

And *that's* when everyone freaked out.

* * *

At first there was a lot of yelling (*"Why didn't you tell us?"*) and disbelief (*"An alien first grader?"*). And of course, Ronnie wanted to see the quincunx up close. But after a while, everyone calmed down.

"So what does this 'Zorcha T'wirpo' character look like?" asked Jason excitedly. "You have to find out, Noah. I bet it's probably gross, like something out of the *Alien* movies."

Jenny shook her head. "You know those movies aren't documentaries, right?"

"Good point. But as Noah's manager, I have to suggest that we try to get some video of T'wirpo. Then we could get it online and use it to monetize our video feed—"

Ronnie raised his hand like he was in class. "But if T'wirpo is really from another p-p-planet, how did the quincunx get *h-here*?" asked Ronnie. "It's impossible."

"He's an alien," I said, like that explained everything.

Ronnie rubbed his bike helmet thoughtfully. "N-Noah, something to th-think about—do you really *know* T'wirpo is an alien from another p-p-planet?" asked Ronnie. "It could just be a c-computer program, like Siri on a s-smartphone."

I almost started arguing with Ronnie, but then realized he had a good point. Since I had no idea what T'wirpo even looked like, it was possible that the "alien" didn't exist at all. Then a really disturbing thought came to me: *Could it all be a trick? Maybe the quincunx ITSELF is Zorcha T'wirpo!*

I gingerly set the quincunx on a stack of board games and eyed it suspiciously.

"What gets me is that your new friend said all of this was for a class project," said Jason. "I don't know if that's awesome or major suckitude."

I kept an eye on the quincunx perched on a chessboard box. *Am I just a pawn in some cosmic game that I don't understand?* "Right now, I'm thinking suckitude," I said. "Major suckitude."

"C'mon, Noah, you got to sh-shoot ice and save those little k-kids," encouraged Ronnie. "That's pretty s-special."

"You have something special too, Ronnie," said Jason with fake seriousness. *"Special pants."*

Ronnie looked down at his dress slacks in surprise. "T-true," he said, smoothing out a crease. Looking at Jason's bright-red sweatsuit, Ronnie frowned as if it hurt his eyes. "If you want, I c-can get some of th-these for you."

35

As the four of us kept talking, two things became clear.

1. Ronnie had no idea he'd just hit Jason with the perfect comeback, and . . .
2. Everyone *really* wanted me to contact T'wirpo.

"It worked once, but I don't want to threaten throwing the quincunx in water again just to get T'wirpo to talk." Perching the disc on my hand, I showed my friends the five-finger method I'd used before. "But nothing happens when I try this now."

Ronnie put his hands on his hips. (Somehow, he could get away with this.) "What if you t-try that with your *other* h-hand?"

I did. Nothing.

"Maybe it's a rhythm thing," said Jenny. "Stick one finger in, then the next finger, and like that."

I put my forefinger in the quincunx's top left hole. "I'm telling you," I said (putting my big finger in the next one) "it's not going" (now my ring finger and pinkie went in the bottom holes) "to work." Lastly, I set my thumb in the center hole.

The quincunx's screen turned red and a song rang out: *"Greetings! You made con-tact! Oh, well done! Please speak to T'wirpo!"*

We all jumped. But even though Jenny was as shocked as the rest of us, she still managed a "told ya."

Despite the song, I assumed I'd be seeing one of T'wirpo's text messages when I tapped the quincunx's screen. Jenny, Jason, and Ronnie moved closer, and then a voice rang out—

"Greetings, No-ah."

I bobbled the quincunx, and Ronnie, Jenny, and Jason all quickly backed away. *It's speaking!*

"Greetings to your companions as well."

The voice was flat, with no emphasis. I couldn't tell how old the speaker was, or even if it was a male or female.

But I *knew* it was T'wirpo. I looked at my friends—I'd never seen their eyes or mouths open so wide. Jenny shook her head a little like she was waking up and whispered, "Ask if there's a way that we can meet."

"That is Jen-ny, yes? In response to your inquiry, it would not be wise."

This brought Jason back to life. He stepped closer and yelled: "Jason here! Hey, if we could see you, we wouldn't be all distracted, wondering what you look like. And it'd also help us understand each other better. So you know, we'd be killing two birds with one stone."

"I have no desire to kill two birds," T'wirpo said. "Not with stones, nor any geological objects."

Jason wasn't discouraged. "Don't worry, it's just a saying. And hey, we earthlings won't judge you if you're all gross and hideous." I made a cutting motion across my throat. Jason gave me a thumbs-up back. "Like, are you slimy, T'wirpo? Do you have tentacles? No offense."

"*Me*, hideous? Ja-son, the first time I saw humans, I was terrified. My parental units had trouble convincing me that you were even intelligent life-forms. No offense."

Now, imagine a barking platypus. That was the sound that came from the quincunx. I couldn't be 100 percent positive, but I was *pretty* sure T'wirpo was laughing.

"Did T'wirpo just trash-talk Jason?" Jenny asked. "I like this alien already."

Then Ronnie—who barely had the nerve to talk to Jenny— spoke up. "Gr-greetings, T'wirpo! Ronnie here. Is it r-rude to ask why we can't t-talk face-to-f-face?"

"It would prove to be a problem." T'wirpo paused. "But excuse me. No-ah, might we please speak alone for a time?"

I mouthed "Sorry!" and pointed to the driveway. The three of them reluctantly trooped out of the garage. "They're gone now. And you're right, we have some serious stuff to talk about."

"I understand," said T'wirpo in a quieter voice than before.

"No-ah, you are aware that powerful forces run our universe, yes? Forces that affect all of us?"

"You mean like gravity?"

"No. I mean forces like *good* and *evil*. My project is designed to see which of these forces is stronger in humans."

"Oh! Well, that's . . . an interesting topic."

"Many intelligent species in the galaxy find humans to be illogical, unpredictable, and violent. And none of us can understand your fascination with frozen yogurt."

"But *you* know we have our good points too."

"True. I believe humans have positive traits, but few agree with me. My schoolmates sometimes taunt me for my affection for your species. Even my best friend has called me 'human brain' and 'people watcher.'"

"They sound mean, T'wirpo."

"Children can be cruel, no matter the species," T'wirpo said with what sounded like a sigh. "But back to my project—I have studied your species' statistics and learned many things about your life expectancy, growth rate, and even brain size. In fact, here is a selection from my report. . . ."

An image appeared on the quincunx screen:

BRAIN SIZE ANALYSIS: *THE HUMANS OF EARTH*

☐ LARGEST BRAINS ON PLANET: ELEPHANTS, WHALES

☐ LARGEST BRAIN SIZE RELATIVE TO BODY SIZE: ANTS (1/7)

THE HUMANS OF EARTH DO NOT HAVE ESPECIALLY LARGE BRAINS. THE RATIO OF BRAIN SIZE TO BODY WEIGHT IS ONE TO FORTY, THE SAME AS A MOUSE. MANY BIRDS HAVE MUCH LARGER RELATIVE BRAIN SIZES (1/14).

CONCLUSION: HUMAN BRAIN SIZE IS UNIMPRESSIVE. FURTHER, THE ORGAN IS INCAPABLE OF EVEN STORING THE FULL VOCABULARY OF LANGUAGE A HUMAN NEEDS TO COMMUNICATE.

"Wow," I said. "You make us sound so lame."

"Yes," T'wirpo agreed. "But statistics are not enough. Observing behavior is important. This is where the quincunx is of use."

I glared at the sparkling quincunx in my hand. "You traitor!" Remember how I'd thought I was being watched when I found it? And here I'd been keeping the spy right in my pocket all along.

I thought back about the way I'd behaved since discovering the quincunx. Sure, I'd made some big mistakes, but overall I'd done more good than harm, right? I mean, the black swifts *were* safe, at least for now.

"My behavior didn't reflect on us humans too badly, right, T'wirpo?"

"It is too early to state. But your adventures have yielded entertainments! For example, your 'peanut butter incident' was replayed many times all over my POO."

I'm a viral star in another solar system!

This meant Jason was closest to the truth when he predicted we were being pranked. "But why make fiery peanut butter, T'wirpo? And why make me float?"

"These decisions are mostly the work of your quincunx. As you know, it is alive, and can act semi-independently."

By now, I believed that T'wirpo really was a "real" alien. But what the alien had just said was something I *couldn't* believe: "So *you* don't take any responsibility for what the quincunx does? That's sad, T'wirpo."

"Yet surely you do not hold a gardener responsible for what his tomatoes do?" demanded T'wirpo.

"Tomatoes don't *do* anything!" I exclaimed. "And if they did, we wouldn't hand them to innocent children."

"Very well. I accept your reproach." T'wirpo paused. "It is true that my species is especially fond of embarrassing events. This may explain the quincunx's choices."

Was I surprised that a seven-year-old alien liked childish comedy? No. But his entire *species*? I imagined what the quincunx's programming checklist looked like:

- ☐ HUMAN SLIPS ON BANANA PEEL, FALLS INTO CEMENT MIXER
- ☐ HUMAN INHALES MARBLE UP NOSE, STAGGERS INTO PATH OF ONCOMING ICE CREAM TRUCK

And despite myself, I smiled. Whatever our differences, it was nice to know we humans had something in common with an alien species.

"No-ah, as I said, our galaxy contains a number of different intelligent species. The majority of them agree that life is rare and should be protected."

This was music to my ears. The aliens were environmentalists!

"There are also rational species that are very dangerous. We use an index to rate these antisocial species. The three with the worst ratings include the Ice Lampreys of Zaltan and the Brain Spiders of Mingrop. These life-forms are intelligent and also quite deadly."

"So everyone wants to be protected from them?" I shivered. *Ice Lampreys!* As scary as they sounded, it was nice knowing that someone was keeping an eye out for universal safety.

"Hey, you said there were *three* monstrous, antisocial intelligent species."

"Yes," said T'wirpo. "The Humans of Earth are the third."

"Wait, what?"

I looked out at my friends in the driveway. *We're monsters!*

Ronnie, Jenny, and Jason looked back. "N-Noah?" called Ronnie. "What's wr-wrong?"

"Oh, nothing." I said weakly. "T'wirpo just wanted to tell me about some stuff. And some other . . . stuff." I looked back at the quincunx, but its screen had vanished. The call must have disconnected right after T'wirpo told me the universe wanted nothing to do with us.

"Right," said Jenny, rolling her eyes. "Let me guess—T'wirpo has a crush on a redheaded alien psycho and needs your expert advice?"

36

THE BLACK SWIFT WHIZZED TOWARD THE WATERFALL. Then, at the last second, it landed on a rock and crawled behind the plunging water.

It must be past three o'clock by now—so where's Sanjay?

Waiting for the mystery kid gave me time to think about what a wild ride I'd been on for the last six days. *I kept saying I didn't want an adventure,* I thought. *But I guess sometimes the adventure finds you.*

A movement on the ground caught my eye. A salamander was slowly making its way to the pool. It was dark purple—almost black—with bright-yellow splotches on it, like paint drippings. As I watched the salamander, a jackrabbit hopped into the canyon.

I looked back, where a coyote was watching me. Then it too loped off in the direction of the jackrabbit.

I felt a surge of pride. I hadn't just saved the black swifts. I'd saved a home for all these animals. But could this home survive on a planet that was run by "monsters"—like me?

A girl suddenly appeared at the trailhead, pushing a powder-blue bike with colored streamers on the handlebars. She propped it on its kickstand and began making weird, exaggerated movements, like she was dancing underwater.

What is *she doing?*

She stretched out an arm, jumped to the side, and waved at her other hand. Then she brought her shoulders up in a contorted shrug. Finally, she shook her hands in the air, ran a few steps, and yelled, "Stupid spiders!"

Oh man, she's just freaking out about a spiderweb.

"Hey." Spiderweb Girl had noticed me. She couldn't have been older than fourth grade, yet she looked vaguely familiar. "You must be the one Sanjay said would be here. What's your name again?"

"I'm Noah. Noah Grow."

"Your first *and* middle names are 'Noah'?"

"No," I said. "Wait, what?"

"You just said your name was Noah Noah Grow."

"No, I meant my name was Noah." I paused. "Noah Grow."

Spiderweb Girl clapped her hands together. "You just did it again!"

Luckily, Sanjay appeared at the trailhead. He was wearing a little backpack and pushing his bright-orange bike up the trail.

Another boy and a girl followed behind, both pushing bikes as well.

Sanjay nodded at me as the three of them parked their bikes behind Spiderweb Girl's. Then the group spread out and formed a half circle around me. Like Sanjay earlier, they all seemed excited, as if something was about to happen.

"Everyone, this is Noah," Sanjay rasped. He shrugged his backpack off and began rummaging around in it. "And I think that Noah has one of . . . *these*." He held up an object he had fished out of his pack.

"No." I staggered backward when I saw it. "That's—that's *impossible*."

There at the end of his robot arm, Sanjay was holding a familiar, glittering device.

A quincunx.

37

I stared at Sanjay's quincunx. Like mine, it was shimmering and iridescent, but where mine was greenish-purple, this one gleamed ocean blue. "That's got to be fake," I whispered.

Spiderweb Girl cocked her head at me. "Why?"

"Because . . . I have the only one!" It sounds silly, but it felt like a betrayal to see a quincunx in someone else's hands.

The other boy, a bony kid in a knit hat, pointed at me. "So you have one too, but you keep it all to *yourself.*"

"Why—I suppose you all share that one?" I asked sarcastically.

"That's right," Knit-Hat Boy confirmed. "We were together when we found it."

"Oh."

"See, all of us got elected as fourth-grade officers," said Sanjay proudly. "I'm class vice president. And Nyla"—he pointed to Spiderweb Girl—"is the fourth-grade webmaster."

"*I'm* president," announced the group's fourth member, a girl with a sequined rainbow on her T-shirt. It seemed like she was going to say more, but a fern distracted her.

Even so, the other three kids were looking at me like they expected something.

"Uh. Congratulations, everyone?"

"Thanks!" Sanjay grinned.

THE LEADERSHIP KIDS *(Cooperativus adolescentia)*

APPEARANCE: A tight-knit group of four student-body officers.

VOICES: Confident and sincere.

PLUMAGE: Varies. Tends toward bright, neon themes.

RANGE: Extremely mobile.

SOCIAL BEHAVIOR: Most members have good interpersonal skills and work well with others.

STATUS: Elected by fellow students, indicating either they have high status—or nobody else wanted their jobs.

Rainbow-T-Shirt Girl looked up from her fern. "The day after that power pole broke, our leadership group went on a field trip to the Hand Fan Museum. And that's where Nyla spotted *that*." She pointed to the blue quincunx in Sanjay's hand.

This is totally unbelievable! "So you're saying there's a whole museum just for hand fans?"

"Yep." Nyla walked over to the pool. Balancing on a jutting rock, she leaned over the water. "I found our Thingy under a palm frond."

"'Thingy'?" I asked.

"That's right," said Knit-Hat Boy. "We figured out how to use it on the bus ride home. So we call it the 'Cooperative Thingy'—or just Thingy."

Nyla held out her hands. "Hey, Sanjay, can you please pass the Thingy over here?"

Sanjay wound up, cocked back his robot arm, and *threw* their Thingy. The glittering blue disc flashed through the air. It was obvious that Sanjay had a good arm but bad aim. Instead of going to Nyla, it hit the rock next to her—

—then, somehow, the Thingy bounced softly off the rock, landing gently in Nyla's hand.

"Whoa!"

"We learned it could do that when I accidentally knocked it off a desk." Nyla tossed the Thingy up and down in her palm. "It's perfectly safe."

Knit-Hat Boy was impatient. "Anyway, where's yours? Sanjay said you were using it in the bathroom. Or do you even really have one?"

I should've been more careful, but that little squirt made me mad. So I yanked my quincunx from my pocket, and held it out. *"See?"*

So yeah, I showed *him*. (No, really. I showed him.)

The kids all leaned forward and "oohed." Even Knit-Hat Boy was impressed.

"So yours is green and purple," Rainbow-T-Shirt Girl said.

"I call it the quincunx," I said. "That's the word for the pattern of five holes on its back."

"Hey, our Thingy has those too," said Sanjay. "When we put our fingers in the back—"

"Dude!" interrupted Knit-Hat Boy. "Let's not tell him *everything*." He looked at me. "So, Noah, have you ever gotten in trouble for using your 'quincunx'?"

Knit-Hat Boy's tone was *so* innocent, it made me wonder. *Why isn't he acting snotty? What's going on here?* Over at the pool, I saw that Nyla had her hands poised over the Thingy— like she was ready to select a command.

I realized the obvious. *This is an ambush!*

Were they going to jump me and try to take my quincunx? Or was Nyla going to use a Thingy menu choice against me?

I was in a tough spot. If I lied about getting in trouble, that could be used against me (and all of humankind) in T'wirpo's report. But if I told the truth, Nyla might zap me with her Cooperative Thingy!

"Um, there've been some hiccups. But overall, finding the quincunx has been . . . a positive experience," I said unconvincingly.

Nyla looked impressed. "I don't know what he just said, but Noah should be in leadership class."

"So you haven't wrecked stuff or broken laws with it?" Man, Knit-Hat Boy didn't give up easily.

"Why would I do that?" I asked in a way that hopefully sounded like *No, I haven't broken the law.*

Sanjay exhaled loudly, and Nyla relaxed and set the Thingy down on the rock beside her. Knit-Hat Boy looked disappointed, though.

"Why?" I asked.

"We just had to be sure," Nyla said, like it was totally obvious.

So these are the good guys? There had been a lot of trouble in Santa Rosa the last few days. It seemed the leadership kids' suspicions had fallen on me. And since they were all about sharing, a person who used a quincunx all by himself must have seemed shady.

"You seem okay, Noah," said Sanjay in his froggy voice.

Behind him, Nyla's handlebar streamers fluttered suddenly in the wind. "I think you should join us."

"Huh? But he wasn't even elected!" protested Knit-Hat Boy. "Besides, he could be a spy or something."

"I'm not a spy," I said.

Knit-Hat Boy pointed at me. "Aha! That's exactly what a spy would say!" Then, seeing that the other leadership kids weren't convinced, he tried a different angle. "Okay, so say Noah did join us. But why? Besides having that quincunx, what's so special about him?"

Mentally, I ticked off a list of things that made me unique.

—I can use chopsticks.
—Sometimes I'll drop my pencil and then catch it before it hits the floor.
—I'm excellent at identifying bird species.
—I know how to play air hockey.

Okay, so it wasn't much of a list. I looked at the group in front of me. Yes, Knit-Hat Boy was annoying, but they all seemed trustworthy. And these kids needed to know the most important thing about their device.

"Let's worry about who's on whose team later," I said. "Right now, I have to tell you where your Thingy came *from*."

"Aliens!" yelled Rainbow-T-Shirt Girl.

I ducked my head and looked around. "Where?"

"She means that aliens made these," explained Sanjay. "They want to destroy us and take our planet."

"Or they want to *enslave* us and take our planet," said Knit-Hat Boy.

"Or they might want to eat us!" chimed in Nyla. "And then take our planet."

T'wirpo never said anything about this *stuff.* "How do you know they want to take the planet? Who told you?"

Rainbow-T-Shirt Girl said, "There was a message on—"

"Nobody needed to tell us," interrupted Knit-Hat Boy. "It's the only thing that makes sense. People couldn't have made these. No matter what the aliens do, we'll be ready."

"So you guys are like a team of little . . . *survivalists*?" I asked.

All four nodded.

Oh boy. I really *need to talk to T'wirpo!*

38

"WOW, WE HAVE A LOT TO TALK ABOUT." I MADE A point of looking at Sanjay's wristwatch. "But first, I need to take a short walk and call home."

"Sure thing." Nyla nodded to Knit-Hat Boy. "But Ricky'll go with you. Things aren't safe right now."

What does that *mean?* I wondered, walking over to the trailhead that led down to my neighborhood. Shadowing me was my fourth-grade bodyguard, Ricky, armed with a knit hat.

"So, Ricky," I said, trying to be friendly, "what did you get elected to?"

Ricky picked up a small dead branch and held it in front of him, one hand at each end. "Class *secretary*," he said, and on the second word, he snapped the branch in two. He threw the broken pieces away and gave me a look, like *Try anything funny and I'll mess you* up.

Ricky was standing uncomfortably close to me. "Look, you don't have to worry about me. I'm not going to run off."

"Yeah?" asked Ricky skeptically. "Well I believe in keeping my friends close—and my enemies closer."

Sheesh! "Wow, I bet your birthday parties are real fun."

Ricky ignored that, but he did wander off a short distance away looking for other sticks to break. As soon as he did, I turned my back and tried the "five-finger rhythm" trick on my quincunx. I tapped the screen and quickly got it up to my ear before the *"Greet-ings!"* song could start.

"T'wirpo!" I whisper-shouted as the connection was made. "I just met a *group* of kids who have their *own* quincunx. Do you want to tell me what's going on here?"

"This is a bolt from the blue!" T'wirpo said. "I had suspected one of my classmates of pilfering my quincunxes—"

"Well, these Earth kids figured out how to use theirs pretty fast," I said quietly. "Look, they haven't communicated with you, have they? It sounded like they got a message."

"No, not from me." Pause. "My hope is that the little earthlings have used their device's *Adeptness* menu but nothing more."

So aliens aren't going to destroy humankind after all.

"That's a relief, T'wirpo. Those kids thought—well, never mind what they thought. I was just worried we were in trouble, after you said we're one of the worst species in the whole *galaxy.*"

Through a gap in the trees, a large, dark, long-winged bird flew past. *Turkey vulture (Cathartes aura)*, I thought absently. "I mean, I was just starting to feel positive about things here."

"Agreed. Let us think in a positive manner, No-ah."

"Sounds good."

"As I wrote in my project report, you humans are the *best* at what you do. No other life-form—not even the Brain Spiders of Mingrop—has ever driven more species on its own home planet to extinction."

"Um . . ."

"You are the champions of thinking of no one but yourselves. For pollution, you win top honors. For destruction, none are your equal—"

"Hang on, hang on," I said. "Sure, we have our problems. But we can't be worse than the *Ice Lampreys*!" I didn't even know what those were, but they sounded horrible.

"The Lampreys *are* pretty bad," T'wirpo admitted.

"I know humans have made some big mistakes," I said. "But we—I mean, my whole species—are still learning how to be responsible. Just look at me! It took me a while to learn how to use the quincunx."

"I believe your species is in a race between your best and worst impulses. And it faces so many questions. For example, can humans survive long enough to colonize outer space?"

"That sounds good."

"It does not sound good to everyone. You see, humans would infest the galaxy."

An infestation of humans? "T'wirpo, if your project results aren't positive, and I—you—we—flunk this ethical test, will it affect your grade?"

"No. My project's results are what is important."

"Good. So if I flunk, it's not the end of the world."

"Not exactly. But your low ethical score *would* add to the evidence for the removal of humans. Many are watching. So please continue behaving as you have been—"

"'Removal'? Wait, what are you saying?" Hearing footsteps running toward me, I paused. "Hang on, T'wirpo." My bodyguard was waving his boney arms around to get my attention. "What's up, Ricky?"

"Noah, we have to go back! *Come on!*" Ricky sprinted up the trail, back to the waterfall.

"T'wirpo? Hello, T'wirpo?" Nothing. I looked at the quincunx, and the screen had disappeared. Did "removal" mean extermination? But T'wirpo said all life is precious and should be protected. Plus, talk about pressure. The way T'wirpo described it, this could be the end of my world . . . and everyone in the galaxy was watching me!

On top of that, the leadership kids were having some kind of emergency. But whatever it was, it couldn't be more important than my news.

My binocs bumped on my chest as I ran after Ricky.

The fourth graders were facing me as I burst into the clearing.

"You guys," I panted, "you're half-right. There *are* aliens, but they don't want to *take over* the Earth. This is all a *test*! And we're failing it—"

Nobody was listening. They were looking up at the sky behind me.

"Noah, can't you smell it?" asked Nyla, pointing.

A thick column of smoke rose above the trees at the trailhead. My heart lurched as I realized what I was seeing. *The extermination program has already begun!* I reached for my scar.

"Is it the aliens?" asked Nyla. "Or is it . . . *her*?" The kids shared a scared look. Even Ricky shuddered.

"Who's 'her'?" I demanded.

"'Her' is the reason we worried about you," said Sanjay. "'Her' is probably who made that power pole by your friend's house fall down."

"Plus, her—I mean *she*—is the one who started that earthquake," said Rainbow-T-Shirt Girl.

I stared. "The earthquake?"

"Yes, the earthquake. Maybe you noticed it?" Ricky was annoyed, but that seemed to be his permanent state. "We know she started it, because we *stopped* it. And we're telling you, aliens want to take over the planet—and they're using people like her to help them."

"If we don't stop her," cried Nyla, "she'll destroy us all!" The other kids looked a little embarrassed. "Okay, sorry about that. Drama class makes me overdo it sometimes."

"But *who* is it we're talking about?" I asked.

"Hi, kids," said a voice from behind us. We whirled around—but nobody was there.

A familiar sound rang out. You know the *Lord of the Rings* movie? There's a part where drumbeats roll out, and they sound like *"DOOM . . . DOOM . . . DOOM."*

That's what we were hearing. *"DOOM . . . DOOM . . . DOOM."*

39

THE WIND CHANGED DIRECTION AND MY EYES STUNG as the air grew gray with smoke. The leadership group huddled closer to Nyla. Grim-faced, she had their Thingy out, ready. Meanwhile, *DOOM, DOOM, DOOM* kept sounding from somewhere above us.

I scanned the trees. "I'm guessing this isn't an orc attack," I whispered.

"We *wish*," said Sanjay.

Something high up in the branches moved. I lifted my binocs—

A *girl*?

She was perched about fifty feet up on the branch of an evergreen tree, with her back to me. And that's where the loud *DOOM*s were coming from!

The girl tapped something round and glittery. The drumbeats stopped. "I'll talk to you later," she said. Then she zipped her backpack and leaped into the air.

"Look out!" I yelled.

She landed easily in a neighboring tree. In the blink of an eye, the girl was climbing down the trunk—not slowly, hugging the tree and picking her way down, but darting like a squirrel, head down and fast. She was almost *dropping*, her hands and feet scrambling on the bark, her mane of hair streaming in front of her.

At the base of the tree, she planted her hands, flipped to her feet, and landed with all her hair flopping over her face.

"Ugh, I hate it when that happens." She whipped her head back. Flaming-red locks of hair fell perfectly into place on her shoulders. "Next time, I'll just braid it."

"Anemona!" *She* was the dreaded "her" the leadership kids were talking about!

She gave a little shrug and looked over at the fourth graders. "Look how adorable you all are!" Anemona made an exaggerated wave at the smoke in front of her face. "Now, I don't know if you children noticed, but there's a fire nearby."

"Yeah, I wonder how *that* started," said Nyla, sarcastically.

"I don't know," warned Anemona. "But in this heat it's going to spread awfully fast. And something tells me that the fire department isn't going to be putting it out."

Nyla leaned into the group and everyone whispered. They quickly reached an agreement. Sanjay looked over. "Noah, we're going to stop that fire. Will you be okay?" He gave Anemona a pointed look.

"I'm sure everything will be fine," I said, unruffled. But I was totally faking it. The fact that Anemona was jumping around with her own quincunx was bad enough. On top of that, it seemed her hobbies were starting earthquakes and setting fires.

And that meant Anemona couldn't be trusted—especially near the black swifts.

As the leadership kids trooped down the trail, I heard Nyla call out, "Be careful. There are like, crazy spiderwebs here."

Anemona waved good-bye, then put her hands on her hips and looked at me. "So, Noah—we're alone at last. Hey, you're the nature expert. Do you know what 'sciurus' means?

I had an idea. "Is it something to do with squirrels?"

"That's it!" Anemona raised her eyebrows and looked impressed. "I had to look that one up when I found it on this." She tapped the quincunx in her bag.

I have to admit something. You already know I had a crush on Anemona. But when she'd stolen my quincunx, she'd crushed my crush. Yet as she stood there, with the smoke swirling around her, Anemona looked like an angel. So I wondered: Was she really all that bad, or was Anemona more like Coby—just misunderstood?

I tried to look tough. "Anemona, tell the truth—did you break the telephone pole in front of the Brights' house?"

"What? No!" she protested. "Didn't woodpeckers weaken

the wood or something? And why would I do that, anyway?"

"Okay, okay." I relaxed a little bit. Call me a sucker, but Anemona's answer actually sounded sincere. "So you probably didn't really have anything to do with the earthquake that hit our school either?"

"Oh, *that.*" And to my astonishment, Anemona laughed and nodded. "I was in a bad mood. Maybe I felt guilty because of what happened with you and Coby. But mostly, we had a test in math that I didn't want to take."

I buried my face in my hands. "You started an earthquake to get out of a *math test*? But it was only worth fifteen percent of your grade!"

"So?" She shrugged. "I only destroyed fifteen percent of the school."

That was exactly the kind of attitude that was giving us humans a bad reputation.

40

"ANEMONA!" I SAID IN A SHOCKED WHISPER. "DON'T talk like that." I tried to quickly explain T'wirpo's project, and how our species was skating on the thin ice of extinction. "See? If we're not careful, it could mean the end of . . . *everything.*"

"Wow, Noah." Her face softened in understanding. "It's like you're speaking to me from your heart."

I nodded, relaxing. *Thank goodness. I think I'm getting through to her.*

"But actually, it's from your *butt.* The only reason things are messed up right now is because of your alien."

"What do you mean?"

Anemona waved her hand dismissively. "You know, this 'Zorcha T'wirpo' character. I heard you in the woods just now, so don't act like you don't know what I mean."

I held up my hand. "Shh!" I said. Anemona's jaw dropped. She wasn't used to being hushed.

Hoo-wett! Hoo-wett!

That squeaky whistling—was it my elusive wood duck? The wind had changed direction again, clearing the smoke enough for me to scan around us. I checked the tree where I'd installed a nesting box. Nope, it was deserted. Then I spotted something—a bird perched on the far side of a dead fir.

If I could just get a good look, I might *finally* be able to check it off my list. . . .

☐ Wood duck *(Aix sponsa)*

I know it seems crazy. But even with everything that was at stake, right then nothing was more important to me than seeing the duck that started my adventures.

I crept across the little canyon with my eyes trained on the bird. I lifted my binocs—but as I did, it hopped to another branch, around the tree trunk.

I eased backward and my hip bumped into something metal—it was Nyla's bike, the one with streamers on the handlebars. It was toppling over, and so was I!

Nyla's bike hit Sanjay's orange bike, and it fell. Two more crashes followed, as the entire row of bikes collapsed like dominoes . . . with me on top!

Wings flapped above me as the bird flew off. I wasn't going anywhere fast, though. I had fallen through Nyla's bike frame with one arm twisted into the chain. That left my other arm and legs sticking up, with my rear end on the ground.

Anemona looked down at me.

"Oops," I said, making a derp face. "Clumsy me."

"Clumsy you," agreed Anemona. "Listen, Noah, I want to talk to you about something. I think we should team up. Between the two of us, we can do amazing things."

This caught me by surprise. "Seriously?"

"Seriously! We can help each other." Anemona held out her hand to me. "Why do you think I set fire to those construction supplies? It was to finish the job that you started—preventing houses from being built here."

I shook my head in disbelief. "But that building project's been cancelled!"

"Really?" She looked up at her smoke plume and laughed. "Oh well—I tried! So just agree to be my partner anyway. Then we can go check on how the kids are doing with that fire. After that—well, think about it, Noah. It'll be SO great. Together, you and I will be able to do whatever we want!"

Anemona said all this in a casual, friendly way. But she was watching me the way a cat watches a sparrow. *What should I do?* In less than an hour, I'd discovered that two other quincunxes existed. One was with Anemona, who saw it as a free ticket for doing anything, at any cost. The other quincunx was with a group of paranoid fourth graders preparing for interplanetary warfare.

Who was scarier—the girl who didn't care about the bigger picture, or the kids who *did* care, but were looking at the *wrong* picture?

I looked at Anemona's outstretched hand and considered her offer. I mean, I did have a lot of things to ask her. After all, based on what Anemona knew, she must have been speaking with an alien, too. But who? What did they talk about? And where had she found her quincunx anyway?

And *squirrel power*?

There was just one problem: Anemona was totally untrustworthy. "I'll pass," I said without moving. (Of course, I *couldn't* move, but still.)

"No? That's too bad." Disappointed, Anemona unzipped her bag and pulled out *her* quincunx. As she tapped at it, I saw it was just like mine, except with a deep metallic ruby glow.

Anemona walked back over to the cliff by the waterfall. "There's a bird nest behind here, isn't there, Noah?" she called innocently before squirrel-ing up the sheer wet rocks.

She wouldn't dare.

Anemona stopped at the exact spot where the black swifts' nest was concealed. "You're the expert, Noah." She reached a hand behind the waterfall and looked back at me. "Do all birds know how to swim?"

She dared!

The baby black swift must have seen Anemona's fingers approaching its home.

Plik-plik-plik?

She has to be stopped! I reached into my shorts pocket and fumbled for my quincunx. A coyote ran past me followed by a jackrabbit. They were fleeing the fire. Overhead, birds were taking to the air, calling out their alarms.

There's already a forest fire, I thought. *Using the quincunx now, especially with an unknown new Adeptness, is a really bad idea. Plus, we're being observed!* That meant that even though Anemona had me trapped, I still had to act ethically. It was a total rip-off, but right now, that meant no quincunx. I had to deal with this crisis myself.

"Noah, I don't have all day," yelled Anemona, while water poured over her arm. "What's it going to be?"

I pushed the quincunx deeper into my pocket. "Okay, okay!" I yelled. "You win!"

A moment later, Anemona dropped down off the cliff, as light as a feather. An evil, evil feather.

She walked over, wet hair dripping down her face, and held out her hand. "Take it." Anemona had double-crossed me, mocked me, destroyed 15 percent of our school, and started a fire. But I didn't see any other way out.

The girl reaching for me just threatened to drown a baby bird, I told myself as Anemona's cold, wet fingers took mine. *And now she's my teammate.*

Perhaps sensing danger, one of the black swifts had returned.

It landed on the waterfall's face. Cocking its head, it looked warily at me with one big, dark eye.

Anemona smiled and she pulled me up and out of the bike trap. "Come on, partner," she said, her green eyes glittering. "Let's go check how the children are doing."

41

It wasn't hard to find the leadership kids. We just followed the sounds of coughing.

Smoldering tree trunks appeared, and the heat intensified as we walked down the trail. Smoke poured from burnt wood, but the flames had been doused and the spot where all the building supplies had been stacked was just empty ashes. In the middle of the burnt ash were four fourth graders.

"Hey, guys!" said Anemona brightly, waving.

Ricky gave Anemona a baleful stare. Nyla cleared her throat. Rainbow-T-Shirt Girl rubbed at a streak of black ash on her rainbow. Sanjay coughed, hunched over with his hands on his knees. I patted his back. "You okay?"

He wiped his eyes and croaked, "Yeah."

"Man, how'd you guys put the fire out so fast?"

Nyla held up the Thingy. "It was easy. We just chose EXTINGUISH."

You've got to be kidding me, I thought.

Without glancing up, Rainbow-T-Shirt Girl said, "There was like a big *'woosh,'* and a weird-smelling wind blew through"—she gestured at the smoking trunks—"and then *this.*"

Ricky must have spotted my incredulous expression. "Looks like Noah's jealous that our Thingy is better than his."

"Isn't that interesting," said Anemona innocently. "Hey, I wonder which one of us has the best one of these . . . 'quincunxes'? Maybe we could have a friendly competition to find out. You know, like a tournament."

The leadership kids were instantly suspicious. "It wouldn't be fair," said Sanjay, managing to get his breath back and straighten up. "It'd be all of us against you."

"Um . . ." I said.

Anemona smiled sweetly. "If anything, it would be Noah and me against YOU. See, we're partners now."

Uh-oh. "Listen, we shouldn't be picking sides—"

"I KNEW IT!" yelled Ricky. He pointed an accusing finger at me. "What have I been telling you guys this whole time?"

The leadership kids drew together, watching Anemona and me warily. Nyla already had their Thingy out and was thumbing through screen selections.

Anemona pulled out her ruby quincunx. "This should be fun," she insisted. "So don't get all carried away with like, winning." She gave me a look. "And, Noah, remember your promise. You're either with me, or you can sit this one out. But no helping *them*."

Argh! I needed to break my agreement with Anemona—but I couldn't. Teaming up with the leadership kids was the right thing to do, but it would be totally unethical. How could something be good and bad at the same time?

As I wrestled with the idea of what to do, something hit me in the back. I turned around as a small rock hit me in the chest. Someone was throwing stuff at me from just beyond the fire circle.

"No-ah," came a whisper from the trees. "Over here!"

I took a few steps toward the trees and whispered back to the phantom rock thrower: "I'm kind of busy right now." But that just caused another rock to sail at me. "Hey, stop it! Who's out there, anyway?"

The voice carried to me from the shadows. "It is me, No-ah. Zorcha. Zorcha T'wirpo!"

* * *

I once read about a dinosaur expert who found a fragment of fossilized bone. That was all she had to go on to reconstruct the animal it came from. Yet after a lot of research, this woman built an entire dinosaur skeleton around that one fragment.

I wasn't trying to build a dinosaur, but I'd been trying to build a picture of what T'wirpo looked like ever since we first "met." There was no fossil, but I did have the quincunx. And also, there was that quick glimpse of what T'wirpo's planet looked like—the quincunx bush and its colorful "fruit" growing beneath four moons.

So till now I'd pictured the alien as either:

—A big, friendly bug . . .

—Or a blue-skinned human-ish being with big, elaborate hair and spotted skin . . .

—Or a plant-eating lizard creature who wore colorful robes.

Guess what?

I wasn't even close.

I stepped out of the fire circle, peered into the shadows of the trees, and saw Zorcha T'wirpo. Finally! The alien was apparently . . . a big ball.

"T'wirpo? Is that you?"

The ball rolled forward and *leaned* toward me, like it was bowing. "Indeed. I am pleased to meet you, No-ah."

ZORCHA T'WIRPO *(Nonterrestria sphaerica)*

APPEARANCE: A greenish-purple sphere about four feet across. No arms, legs, tentacles, or heads are visible. Closer inspection reveals the ball's surface is semi-transparent. Beneath that surface, shapes and patterns move slowly, like Jupiter's gas clouds.

VOICE: Speaks each word with the same volume and emphasis.

PLUMAGE: None.

RANGE/SOCIAL BEHAVIOR: Moves by rolling around like a big bubble of mercury. Exact range unknown, but undoubtedly far-reaching. Behavior suggests sociability with other species.

STATUS: Unknown.

So this is it. I gulped. *The first meeting ever between humans and aliens. And who's the human ambassador making a connection from our little planet to the stars? Who has this awesome responsibility?*

ME.

Whatever words I said next would go down in history. They'd be included along with other legendary lines, like "I have a dream" and "That's one small step for man, one giant leap for mankind." Who knows? Maybe schoolkids centuries from now would learn about what was said here today.

Here's what I went with:

"Dude—you're a *ball*?"

"A ball?" T'wirpo rolled backward a little. "No-ah, I am not a ball any more than you are a doll."

Even in sci-fi films, I'd never even seen anything quite like T'wirpo. *All those people who imagined extraterrestrials as human beings with bad hair and weird skulls should be embarrassed,* I thought. *Like me!*

T'wirpo seemed to find me just as strange. "I am fascinated by that wet cave residing in your face," the alien said. "The large one you call the 'mouth.' I trust this is not rude, but do you find it difficult to use that cave for both speaking as well as eating?"

I ran my tongue over my teeth. "It sounds weird when you say it that way, but I guess you get used to it. So where is your, um, eating cave?"

T'wirpo spun. The mottled layer under its red skin moved independently. I realized why T'wirpo didn't want to meet "face-to-face." T'wirpo didn't seem to have one! (A face, that is.)

Meanwhile, T'wirpo had finished turning. "There. But I am afraid you cannot see my eating cave because of the PEE."

"What?"

T'wirpo spun again, although his front and back seemed identical. "No-ah, I am wearing a protective suit. The Planet Earth Enabler. My PEE protects me from Earth's low gravity, high temperature, and your toxic gases, like oxygen."

Aha! So as a space suit just sort of suggests what the human inside looks like, I wasn't seeing the "real" Zorcha T'wirpo. What I was seeing was its . . . PEE.

Still, I had to ask. "T'wirpo, do you know what 'pee' means here on Earth?"

"Allow me to check my database . . . ah, it is 'bodily waste water'? First POO and now PEE." I jumped back as the alien barked. "I have done it again!"

"I hate to even ask, but where *do* you get rid of waste?"

The alien just looked at me. (I know, it didn't have eyes, but still.)

"Waste?" I added. "Poop?"

"I do not know what you are trying to get at."

I sighed. "Okay, let's try this. You can obviously see, but where are your eyes?"

Imagine a big ball nodding. "My vision receptors are in my skin, all around me. For example, I see that two of your friends are approaching at this very moment."

Jason and Ronnie burst out of the trees behind T'wirpo, and Jason launched right in: "What the heck, Noah? A fire? I thought everything was supposed to be okay now!" Then he noticed T'wirpo. "And why are you hanging out with an exercise ball?"

Always the soccer player, Jason tried to kick the "ball" out of the way. As he did, T'wirpo squished down—and then bounced high up in the air.

A moment later, T'wirpo gently landed, its bottom flattening and then returning to shape. "Please refrain from that, Ja-son," T'wirpo said. "I understand your confusion, but I am not an apparatus for one of your sporting matches."

"Guys," I said, "meet T'wirpo, the quincunx grower from an unknown POO."

Jason's jaw went slack. His eyes rolled. And his limbs flopped, one by one, like a marionette whose strings were being cut.

"He's f-f-fainting!" cried Ronnie.

I *almost* caught Jason before his head hit a log.

42

Jason's eyes flickered open.

"What happened?"

"You f-f-fainted," said Ronnie. "Then you hit your head on a l-log."

T'wirpo rolled worriedly around the three of us. "Is Ja-son reaching peak health again? Or is this an emergency of grave import? Your facial ingredients are very confusing."

Jason looked over. "Our facial ingred—you mean our *expressions*?" He rose unsteadily to his feet, and I could tell Jason was a little disappointed T'wirpo didn't have any slime or tentacles.

"It is good to meet both of you in person." T'wirpo did one of its little bows. "Especially, you, Ron-nie. You are one of the few humans who does not pain my sight receptors."

"It's because of his pants, isn't it?" asked Jason, still rubbing his head.

"No, said T'wirpo. "It is because Ron-nie's shape is pleasingly spherical."

I was getting nervous. "Look, I could stand here and talk about Ronnie's awesomeness all day, but shouldn't we go check on those other two quincunxes?"

And as if in answer, a deep drumbeat sounded through the smoldering tree trunks:

DOOM . . . DOOM . . . DOOM.

We raced toward the *DOOMs* inside the burn zone. (Well, *three* of us raced, one rolled.) Anemona had answered her call and was holding her red quincunx to her ear. "All right, then," she said. "Yes, I'll see you soon."

Amenoma glanced at T'wirpo, the *rolling alien* (!), then casually looked around the clearing as if there might be something more interesting out there. I followed her gaze—and watched a large red ball shoot from the woods, skipping fast over the ground toward us, like a flat rock on water.

"An alien!" Nyla yelled. Then she spotted T'wirpo. "*Round aliens!*" The leadership kids' heads turned back and forth between T'wirpo and this newcomer as if they were watching extraterrestrial tennis. All of the kids—even Rainbow-T-Shirt Girl—wore grim determined looks, like: *our time has come.*

As for Anemona, she was like a hostess on a game show. "Everyone, please meet . . . um, would you pronounce your name for us?"

The red ball bounced slightly. "Florcha Y'tofer!" The voice vibrated with excitement. Its red PEE seemed smaller than T'wirpo's, and the mottled patterns beneath the ball's surface moved more quickly.

I looked over at T'wirpo, whose green PEE had faded to a pale yellow. "Hey, do you know Y'tofer?"

T'wirpo rolled uneasily back and forth. "Indeed—but we are not exactly friendly companions. In fact, one could say that Y'tofer is my 'Coby.'"

The leadership kids began pointing to the opposite side of the fire circle. *What now?* And as if a forest fire and two aliens weren't distracting enough, yet *another* ball emerged from the woods.

Ricky actually looked disappointed. "Earth is being invaded by a bunch of beach balls?"

As the new alien entered the burn zone, it didn't roll along like T'wirpo or bounce through the air like Y'tofer. Instead, it skittered sideways around burnt trunks, and almost daintily sidestepped fallen branches. (I know, the ball didn't actually *step*, but it seemed to.)

It rolled to a stop a short distance from us, close to the leadership kids. This new sphere was sky blue, and looked a bit larger than T'wirpo. Then it made a sound like popcorn popping. Some pops were deep and slow, and others sounded like drumsticks rolling on a snare.

T'wirpo's PEE regained a little of its green color. "Let us

speak in a manner these Earthlings understand. What are you doing here, Morcha Ph'pyp?"

Despite its round shape, the alien named Ph'pyp somehow shrugged in a way that communicated annoyance and guilt. "Very well," the blue sphere answered. "As I was saying, T'wirpo, your planet smells like Jadrockian garbage."

"Wow, that's some b-body language," said Ronnie, impressed.

"Yes," said T'wirpo in an aside. "Shrugging is a primary part of my best friend's communication."

"*That's* your best friend?" Jason did a fist pump. "We're saved! It's two against one!"

"I have come out of respect to our friendship, T'wirpo," continued Morcha Ph'pyp. "That, and because my parental units made me." The sphere gave another shrug, and this one somehow said, *Now I have to do something I don't want to.* "First, my confession—I harvested one of your quincunxes. At the time, I did not know Y'tofer had plucked one as well.

"I deposited this quincunx in a human museum in the belief that a reasonably civilized earthling would find it." Ph'pyp spun slowly toward the fourth-grade leadership kids. "This was apparently an error. Even so, I am responsible for my actions—and by extension, for these earthling primates."

Then the ball rolled sideways a little closer to the leadership kids, who recoiled in horror. (Well, all of them except for Rainbow-T-Shirt Girl, who was dabbing at the ash on her shirt again.)

"But why?" T'wirpo shuddered from some emotion. Was it anger? Surprise? Confusion? "Why would you do such a thing, Ph'pyp?"

"It was a small-minded and mischievous act." The blue sphere's color deepened defiantly. "But, T'wirpo, your 'save the humans' interest has come to exclude all other activities. Can you even recall the last time we played with the Albian Proto-Matter Creator? We never even clamber together on a simple Möbius Fun Climb—"

I jumped as if stung by a bee. "My parents invented that!"

Ph'pyp turned toward me. I got the feeling it was giving me a look like I was an unpleasant bacteria in a microscope. "One of your species' rare contributions to culture. You humans—you live in a vast, unknowable galaxy of infinite beauty. So what do you name it?"

Sanjay raised his hand and started jumping up and down. "Ooh, I know! The Milky Way!"

"Yes, the Milky Way," confirmed Ph'pyp sarcastically. "You compare the most amazing thing imaginable to a dairy product. Why not simply call our galaxy the Small Curd Stars, or Frozen Yogurt Vista? Perhaps then the Interstellar Community will welcome you with open limbs."

Rainbow-T-Shirt Girl took a halting step towards Ph'pyp, which I thought was pretty brave.

"Listen, I'm a peer counselor," she said. "What I hear you saying, Ph'pyp, is that your feelings got hurt when your best friend ignored you. So you did something hurtful that you'd like to apologize for."

Ph'pyp froze. The alien may have traveled across the vast void of the galaxy, but nothing had prepared it for Rainbow-T-Shirt Girl.

But right then, I just felt bad for Zorcha T'wirpo. Here this little extraterrestrial had tried to do the right thing by us humans, only to be betrayed by its best friend. And on top of that, T'wirpo's worst enemy, Y'tofer, was deliberately messing up its science project. Its *really important* science project!

"Hey, T'wirpo," I said softly. "Are you okay?"

T'wirpo's sphere slumped. "This has been both a great shock and a mammoth disappointment."

"But all three quincunxes are here, right now. Just take them back!"

"The quincunxes bond with their harvesters. So while I can communicate with yours, No-ah, only my classmates here can influence the other two—"

"Behold," interrupted Ph'pyp, sounding unimpressed. "Another human."

Red-faced and straining, Jenny appeared. She was forcing her wheelchair over the uneven, ashy ground with brute strength.

"I should have known she wouldn't miss this," muttered Jason.

He and Ronnie ran to her, and the two helped push Jenny

from behind. As they did, Jason talked fast to bring his sister up to speed on the situation.

Meanwhile, Y'tofer started bouncing up and down, scattering ashes into the air.

"Okay everyone," Anemona announced. "Y'tofer is totally bored, and so am I." She looked meaningfully at the leadership kids. "So *we* say it's time to get this tournament started. Like, right NOW!"

Sanjay's eyes widened. "Hang on—what are the rules?"

Anemona glanced at her ruby quincunx. "There's only one rule—you use your little Thingymabob and I'll use mine. And we'll see whose is better."

"I'd like to know a few m-more details first," Ronnie said. "For example, is this tournament dangerous? Are w-we all going to get killed?"

Jason was totally in his element. "We'll be *fine!*" he coached. "We just need to have the right attitude for it. Tell me, people— are we ready to kick butt and take names?"

"I think w-we already know everyone's names," Ronnie pointed out. "Or is the idea to k-k-kick people's butts and keep track of their names as we go? That way, we have a l-l-list of whose butt was kicked and whose wasn't."

Jason rubbed his forehead. "Yes, Ronnie. We're all going to get killed."

As we wasted precious time, Nyla waved for the leadership kids and Ph'pyp to huddle around her. A quiet argument began—Ricky and Rainbow-T-Shirt Girl wanted to choose a menu item from the Thingy right away, while Ph'pyp, Sanjay, and Nyla said to wait and see what Anemona and I did first.

"Hey, you guys!" I called over and held up my quincunx. "Remember, I'm not against you!"

They all ignored me, except Ricky. He gave me a hand gesture. (It wasn't a very nice one.)

As for Anemona and Y'tofer, they must've already chosen, because the redhead and the red ball were just staring up at the sky.

Ominous dark clouds appeared.

"Hey, do you feel that?" asked Jenny. I *did* feel it—the air crackled with energy. You know that weird sensation of rubbing a balloon on wool? Multiply that by fifty.

"Nyla, hurry!" Sanjay urged, looking up at the clouds. "Just pick something!"

"Hey, Anemona, my money is on those kids and Mr. Grumpy over there!" Jenny called out, as the static made her dyed green hair rise. "What's so great about what you chose?"

Anemona's eyes danced. "Oh nothing, if you don't count the LIGHTNING!"

"What?" I exclaimed. *Is she out of her mind?* "I thought this was just for fun!"

Pointing a hand up at the gathering storm clouds, Anemona gave a delighted laugh. "IT IS!"

43

"Did you hear that, T'wirpo?" I demanded. "She gets LIGHTNING, but I have—" I scrolled, but my quincunx's menu was completely empty. "*Nothing.*"

T'wirpo sat silently as the clouds swirled together, grew darker, and sank lower. Anemona raised her other hand, as if she were holding a sledgehammer. A flash of light sparked above, arcing across the sky.

Anemona looked at Ph'pyp and the leadership kids, then swung her imaginary sledgehammer down! Lightning streaked toward the doomed group, just as they all disappeared beneath—

A giant bowl.

Okay, it wasn't an *actual* bowl. It was some kind of protective dome, but it looked like a big ceramic bowl turned upside down. The leadership kids' Thingy must have offered it as a defensive choice.

The bowl's curved surface glowed as the fork of lightning struck, but it held firm. A micro-instant later, a bigger lightning bolt hit in the exact same spot. This strike made the bowl shimmer so brightly, I had to close my eyes—and then the thunderclap hit!

I squeezed my hands over my ears but could still feel the force of that crash of thunder shaking my whole body. While my eyes were shut and my ears were covered, something gently bumped into my hip.

It was T'wirpo! "No-ah," the alien said. T'wirpo's color had now completely returned to its original greenish-purple. "Please check your quincunx."

I did—and fast. Two items, HOMING and SEQUESTRATE, appeared on the list.

Now what? I'd gone from no choices to having one too many. "You guys, I have two things to pick from—HOMING and SEQUESTRATE. Which one should I take?"

"Take the second one," said Jason. "I mean, the other one sounds like it's for homing pigeons."

"Maybe HOMING homes in on a person's weakness, and then uses it against them," suggested Jenny.

This wasn't helping. Anemona was winding her arms up again in a pretty good Thor imitation. "Hey, kids!" she yelled at the leadership kids' dome. "I'm starting to get the hang of this!"

T'wirpo tilted back to observe the storm clouds. "It appears the red-haired human is packaging a number of lightning strikes into a single, more powerful one."

The bowl shielding Ph'pyp and the leadership kids was already scorched all over, and I could see a fine, jagged crack across the top. It didn't look like it could survive another lightning strike.

Ronnie must have seen it too. Before Anemona could unleash the fury of the heavens, he howled, "*STOP!*" Except it was all drawn out, like "*STOOOOOP!*"

Amazingly, everyone did. Stop, I mean. Even the storm clouds seemed to hold still for a moment. Ronnie—quiet little Ronnie—had just yelled!

"Anemona, Y'tofer—you can't do this," Ronnie said. "We humans have inalienable rights!"

Did you notice the amazing thing about that? *Ronnie didn't even stutter.*

"'Inalienable rights'?" asked Anemona. "What does that even mean?"

Ronnie coughed. "W-w-well, I actually just heard it in a m-movie somewhere."

Anemona gave him a disgusted shake of her head and went right back to her thunder goddess routine.

So now it was up to me. HOMING and SEQUESTRATE were right there on my quincunx, but which one could stop a thunderbolt?

"Hey, Noah—why not pick both of them?" asked Jenny.

Yeah, I thought. *Why not?*

Taking Jenny's suggestion, I used two fingers to select both commands at the same time. After tapping my quincunx's side, its screen flashed back and forth between two commands:

HOMING

SEQUESTRATE

HOMING

SEQUESTRATE

Suddenly I felt like nothing could touch me. Literally!

Do you remember the sucking feeling I got when I used EXPROPRIATE? The new sensation sweeping through me was the exact *opposite* of that. It was like I was a refrigerator magnet that had been turned around and was invisibly pushing other magnets away.

When I'd used the quincunx before, it'd affected particular parts of my body, like my hands and mouth. But I wasn't sure how to channel this new "repelling" sensation—it seemed to be radiating out from my whole body.

Lightning arced between the clouds above us. It looked like the next thunderbolt Anemona called down was going to be totally fearsome. There was no way the leadership kids' dome could handle it.

"Okay, Noah," said Jason. "It's time to kick butt!"

"And don't f-f-forget the names," Ronnie.

Like a baseball pitcher, Anemona finished her windup and prepared to call down her thunderbolt. . . .

So I looked right at her—and I released all that HOMING/ SEQUESTRATE from inside of me! Gauzy energy surged out from my whole body, flowing in all directions. As the first wave hit Anemona, her eyes locked with mine for one terrible second.

"Backstabber!" she howled, and then Anemona was gone.

If we watched a super slow-mo replay, you could see that Anemona didn't just *poof* disappear. Instead, it was like she suddenly flew backward to a distant spot, like at the far end of a telescope.

Then she was gone.

At the same time, there was also a shrinking red blur from behind Anemona, as Y'tofer went with her down the end of the telescope.

"Yeah!" I held back on the next wave of HOMING/ SEQUESTRATE, and the gauzy energy surge dissolved into the air. "Did you guys see that?"

There was no answer. "Guys?"

I turned to find Ronnie, Jason, Jenny, and T'wirpo were all gone. Not only that, but the dome over Ph'pyp and the leadership kids had *also* vanished—along with everyone beneath it!

"Anyone?" There was no way they'd had time to run off.

So that meant that HOMING/SEQUESTRATE had flowed out from me in ALL directions, sending each person and alien down the wrong end of the telescope, one after another.

"Hey!" Nyla's head popped up from the ground. Then she stood and stepped out of the small furrow she'd been lying in. *Nyla must have dropped down into it after their dome appeared,* I thought. *And being underground protected her from* HOMING/SEQUESTRATE.

Nyla patted her pockets down, then started to search the ground nearby. "Noah," she said, glancing over, "where'd everyone go?" I must have looked guilty, because Nyla added, "Did you *do* something to them?"

"Probably. I mean, I don't really know," I admitted, pressing my quincunx's stem and feeling the energy inside me die down. "But whatever happened, it was an accident."

"So you 'accidentally' did *something*, and now all my friends and all your friends are gone?" Nyla gave me a wary look. "Ricky was right about you." With that, she ran off toward Noyd Falls.

"Nyla, wait!" I yelled, running after her.

She didn't.

Alone in the silence, I looked up and watched the dark storm clouds separate from each other and scatter to the wind. Then . . . well, there's no non-awkward way to say this—I felt something in my shorts. Like, added weight that wasn't there before.

(No, not *that*.)

Reaching into my right pocket, my fingers met something

smooth and oval. Pulling it out, I found a ruby-colored quincunx. Anemona's! And in my left pocket, I found the leadership kids' blue Thingy.

This is what Nyla was looking for, I realized. *So now I've got all THREE quincunxes. But how?*

My best guess was that SEQUESTRATE probably meant something like "confiscate." But that only explained part of the puzzle. I'd also just sent a whole group down the telescope. (Luckily, they hadn't ended up in my pockets.) Had HOMING sent them to *my* home? That could be a problem. Sure, my parents are easygoing. But having three aliens rolling around in our backyard might freak even Mom and Dad out—even if the aliens *were* fans of the Möbius Fun Climb.

Of course, HOMING could have just sent everyone to their *own* homes. *Yeah,* I thought, crossing my fingers. *That's probably what it did.*

Otherwise, I might have just sent seven innocent kids to an alien space station—or even a distant planet. (Okay, *five* innocent kids, plus Ricky and Anemona.)

Just as I reached the waterfall, I glimpsed Nyla pushing her bicycle down the trail quickly, her handlebar streamers flying behind her.

But were the twins safely home again? The only way to find out was to get to the Brights' home right away! I was worried, but the weight of the quincunxes in my pockets somehow reassured me a little. After all, I had all *three* of them. With the powers they contained, I could fix this problem. Really, I could fix *any* problem, right? True, it's not like I needed to unleash an earthquake, smite something with lightning, or freeze a swimming pool right at that moment.

But just knowing I *could* do those things was a pretty awesome feeling.

The flap of deep wing beats suddenly filled the air. A colorful bird circled the pool, gleaming shades of green and purple shining from its feathers as it glided down onto the water.

That crested head, those colors . . . WOOD DUCK!

Ripples surged in the water from the force of the drake's landing. A frog jumped into the water with a splash, which led to a series of splashes as other startled frogs launched into the pool. Each splash created a ripple of its own, and so another frog, and another, would launch itself into the water.

Ripples within ripples. Causes and effects. Dominoes in an infinite sea of darkness.

And *that* made me think that I needed to wise up! Having all three quincunxes only guaranteed one thing—the twins were in trouble.

I began digging a hole near the pool with a stick and my hands. As I did, the wood duck paddled contentedly around, bobbing its head back and forth. I dug deeper and deeper. At last, I set the three quincunxes—one blue, one ruby red, and one purple-green—into it.

"You'll be safe here," I said. I covered the hole, then I moved a flat rock over the spot.

As I stood, the drake tipped forward, plunging his head underwater, and pushing its upended rump straight up.

Despite everything, I smiled.

☑ Wood duck (*Aix sponsa*)

Then, just to hear the name out loud, I said it. "Wood duck."

The drake popped up from the water and gazed over with its majestic red eyes.

The bird's watching the bird-watcher and the bird-watcher's watching the bird, I thought, glancing at the sky. *And T'wirpo— are you up there again, watching us?*

With a sudden flap of its wings, the drake flew onto a nearby tree, landed on a branch, and perched next to *another* bird. She was brown with white spots and a crested head. A female wood duck.

Then I saw the nesting box—the one I'd installed last year— was in that tree. It looked like I'd attracted a pair of wood ducks, after all. Maybe next spring, the nesting box would be full of ducklings.

My spirits lifted. Yes, there were ultra-serious questions facing me, my friends, and the whole planet. But you know what? It looked like my Drake Equation had possibility. That meant maybe there was still hope for Zorcha T'wirpo's project, too.

I needed to get moving, so I started down the trail. I had to find Ronnie and the twins and everyone else. (Yes, even Ricky!)

Behind me, the water bubbled and the ducks nestled in together. The three quincunxes rested quietly together. And in a hidden nest behind the waterfall, a healthy little black swift called out:

Plik-plik-plik-plik.

Acknowledgments

Writing this story would have been impossible without the help of Django Jacobsen Fein, Holden Hindes, Marian Davis, Ricardo Mejías, and Aaron Judd. Thank you! And a tip of the cap to Kira Porton, Pam Erlandson, Robert Rowzee, Vianne V. Wagner, Tina Nichols Coury, Cindy Loh, and the staff at both the Reed College Library and Portland's Hollywood Library. Extra-special thanks to my wife, Lynn, to my sister, Mary Zephrinia King, and to all the good people at the Audubon Society of Portland.

I wouldn't be writing at all if it weren't for the inimitable Suzanne Taylor. Nor would this story have seen the light of day without my superlative agent, Jill Corcoran. Finally, editor extraordinaire Tracey Keevan has my deep appreciation for her insight and diligence.

Now, a Fun Fact! The inspiration for this book came from a young man named Noah Thorin King-Groh. (He's cool.)